WALTER DEAN MYERS

SLAM!

S0-ABB-158

POINT

SCHOLASTIC INC.

New York Toronto London Auckland Sydney
Mexico City New Delhi Hong Kong Buenos Aires

To Grace Killens, with thanks for her support.

ISBN 0-590-48668-3

12 11 10 9 8 7   6 7 8/0

Printed in the U.S.A.   01

Praise for
WALTER DEAN MYERS'S
SLAM!

■ "[An] admirably realistic coming-of-age novel"
— *Booklist,* boxed review

"A Harlem teenager learns how to apply the will he
has to win at hoops to other parts of his life in this
vivid, fluent story....Few writers can match Myers for
taut, savvy basketball action."
— *Kirkus Reviews*

"Readers will appreciate *Slam!* for the honesty with
which Myers portrays the dreams of one Harlem
teenager."
— *The Horn Book*

"Enduring truths, winningly presented"
— *Publishers Weekly*

"Once again, Myers produces a book that reinforces
his standing as a preeminent YA author."
— *School Library Journal*

"Open to any page, and let Myers's skill with words
pull you into the story. *Slam!* will fly off the shelves
into the hands of basketball fans, and will give them a
lot more than a game."
— *Voice of Youth Advocates*

"Myers has a neat trick of making the reader see the world through Slam's streetwise, life-naïve eyes....The conclusion is hopeful, and the basketball scenes are tough."

— *Bulletin of the Center for Children's Books*

A Coretta Scott King Award Winner

An American Library Association Best Book for Young Adults

A New York Public Library Book for the Teen Age

An American Library Association Quick Pick

Basketball is my thing. I can hoop. Case closed. I'm six four and I got the moves, the eye, and the heart. You can take my game to the bank and wait around for the interest. With me it's not like playing a game, it's like the only time I'm being for real. Bringing the ball down the court makes me feel like a bird that just learned to fly. I see my guys moving down in front of me and everything feels and looks right. Patterns come up and a small buzz comes into my head that starts to build up and I know it won't end until the ball swishes through the net. If somebody starts messing with my game it's like they're getting into my head. But if I've got the ball it's okay, because I can take care of the situation. That's the word and I know it the same way I know my tag, Slam. Yeah, that's it. Slam. But without the ball, without the floorboards un-

1

der my feet, without the mid-court line that takes me halfway home, you can get to me.

So when Mr. Tate, the principal at my new school, started talking about me laying low for the season until I got my grades together I was like seriously turned out. The night after he talked to my moms I couldn't sleep. It wasn't the hissing of the radiator or my little brother talking in his sleep in the other bed, it was the idea of not playing ball that was bouncing crazylike through my head.

Sometimes I don't mind not sleeping. I like to lay in the dark and listen to the sounds coming up from the street. I can lay in bed and tell just what time it is by how much traffic go by in the street below. When it's late night you hear the sound of car doors and people talking and boom boxes spilling out the latest tunes. When it rains the tires hiss on the street and when there's a real rain with the wind blowing sometimes you can hear it against the tin sign over Billy's bicycle shop. If there's a fight you hear the voices rising and catching each other up. The sound of broken glass can cut through other noises, even if it's just a bottle of wine somebody dropped. And behind all the other sounds there's always the sirens, bringing their bad news from far off and making you hold your breath until they pass so you know it ain't any of your people who's getting arrested or being taken to the hospital. In the early morning you hear the clang of the garbage trucks, then the low growl of the buses and you know the people who got work are starting off downtown to their jobs.

In the morning you don't hear any police sirens or ambulances. It's like all the shooting and chasing is over for the night and the neighborhood is getting ready for a new day. You hear the news on the radios of people who got a reason to get up early and you hear mamas yelling for their kids who go to school to wake up. Soon as the first radio goes on in the morning, Salty, the pit bull Akbar keeps in his shop, wakes up and starts howling. Salty is a trip. He can do his regular howl, which ain't much, or he can howl like a police siren or an ambulance. Whatever way he howls you know what's coming down the street long before you get to see it.

When something bothers me a lot I keep thinking about it, like I'm replaying a tape over and over. No matter what I do it stays in my head.

I must of dozed off and woke up still thinking about my moms coming to school the day before. She's cool. She come to Mr. Tate's office and listened to him talk about how he was so disappointed in me. He was saying it like he knew me, but he was calling me Gregory instead of Greg, which is my name. Greg Harris. No way he would be into Slam.

When Mr. Tate asked my moms did she know how I was doing in my subjects, she said yes, and that I would do better. The way she said it was firm, but her eyes were glistening and I knew she was hurt by what he was saying. She really wanted me to do good. She didn't look at me, which made me feel bad.

When she left, Mr. Tate ran the whole thing down to me again about how I was going to fail this subject or I was going to fail that subject and how later on I wouldn't be able to get a good job. He said it slow like maybe he thought I wouldn't get it if he said it too fast. I got it all right, I just couldn't do nothing with it.

When I got home Moms made some tea, which is what she always does when things get serious. That was together because I know she's definitely in my corner and I knew things were serious so I sat with her and we had the tea and she talked about how she had it when she went to school in Brooklyn. Then my pops come in with Derek. Derek's nine years old and got more mouth than he got backup. He's always running up the stairs with some dude on his tail ready to bust him up. But you can't be mad at him because he got this stupid grin that's crooked and when he flashed that grin at you and you started grinning back you just couldn't hold on to being mad. I worry about him, though. I'm seventeen and the streets mess with me and keep me nervous, and he's only nine.

He saw the conversation going on and come in and parked himself on the couch. I figured Pops would be in on the gig in a minute, too.

Me and Moms and Derek are like real family; so is Pops when he's acting right, which means when he's working. When he's working he's like laid back at home and he's mostly off the bottle. He takes a little taste now and then, but it's no big thing. And every job he gets it's supposed to be this big position and you know it's not that much, but he's scoping and hoping so you go along with it. When he's not working he gets into these moods and sometimes he gets nasty. He drinks hard, too. Sometimes he and Moms split up, but they always get back together. She digs the dude, and so do we.

Funny thing is that Derek looks a lot like Moms and I look like I'm in between them. Mom is round and you could tell she was fly back in the used to be. Pops is thin and nervous-looking. Sometimes when he's down he sits in the dark with

5

his eyes open. I can understand him not being cool when he doesn't have a job.

"Mama came home crying," Derek said.

"Yo, man, why don't you shut up!" I said.

"Why he got to shut up?" my pops asked, coming into the room wiping his hands on a paper towel. "You the one made your mama have to go round to the school. You the one the principal talking about. Why Derek got to shut up?"

"He don't have to shut up," I said. I got up from the couch.

"I'm going to have supper ready soon," Moms said. "I'm just waiting for the rice to finish cooking."

"I'm not hungry," I said.

"You got to have a balanced diet," Derek piped up again. "If you don't you can grow funny."

If Derek makes ten it's going to be a miracle.

I went to the room me and Derek shared, laid across the bed and tried to chill, but I knew it wasn't going to work. The mess was just working on my cap like a bad toothache or something. Mr. Tate talking about "don't I know how I hurt my mother?" Man, she's sitting up in his office fixing to cry and whatnot and he asking some stupid mess like that.

Mr. Tate had thrown in a remark about how I might have to transfer back to Carver if my grades didn't turn around. The way he said it was as if there was something wrong with Carver. I liked Carver. It was just that when they had all the fuss about getting more black kids to go to the magnet schools I got picked to go to Latimer for visual arts. Everybody had talked about how dope Latimer was. It was okay, but it wasn't all that.

The bedroom door opened and Moms came in with some fried chicken, green beans, rice, and gravy.

"I'm not hungry," I said again.

"This isn't for you," Moms said. "This is my food. I just thought I'd come in here and eat it while I talked to you."

"Oh."

"You think any more about what Mr. Tate said?"

"You know I did," I said.

"He mentioned you giving up the art club and basketball and using the time for studying." She had the plate on her lap.

"I don't know. What this school is all about is doing stuff. Everybody's in a band, or in a club," I said. "If I got to act like I'm in jail I might as well go on back to Carver."

"You sure you don't want part of this chicken?"

"If you're just going to sit there and hold it . . ." I said.

"Baby, I know it's hard," Moms said, handing me the plate. "Those kids at Latimer have been doing well for a long time. You got to catch up. You know what I mean?"

"You think I should give up everything and just study?"

"How about giving up one of them," Moms said. "Either leave the art club or don't go out for basketball."

"What did Pops say when I left?"

"He didn't say much more," Moms said. "Don't get gravy on my spread."

"Yes, ma'am."

"But you know how he feels," she went on. "He just wants you to do good."

"Yeah, I know. Maybe I'll give up the art club."

"I didn't think you could stand walking away from basketball." Moms got up and went to the door. "When you finish eating, bring the plate out to the kitchen and wash it. I don't want any roaches in here."

"Yo, Mom, you mind if I punch out Derek tonight?"

"Don't you hit Derek," she said. "He's the only cute child I got."

8

Sometimes I set stuff up in my mind like it's going to be true, even though in my heart I know it's not true. It's when I want something so bad it gets real to me before it even happens. I could see me doing this with the basketball tryouts. I mean, like, I knew that nothing I did on the basketball court was going to get my grades up and everything, but somehow I still had this vision of me busting out on the court and then everything being all right. It didn't make sense, but there it was.

The gym's on the fourth floor and when I get there I see the tryouts are already going on.

"Didn't you read the notice?" this kid says to me. "Tryouts began at two-thirty."

I took out the notice and checked it out. It did say two-thirty. I knew it when I first read it, but then I kind of switched it in my mind so that I made it seem like after school. No big deal.

I put on my sweats and shoes and sat on the bench. Mr. Goldstein was the assistant coach and he told the regular coach, Mr. Nipper, that I was there to try out. Coach, he just looked over at me and looked away.

They had set up a game. Mr. Goldstein was the ref and Coach Nipper was sitting down on the sidelines taking notes. They had five guys playing on each side, shirts and skins, and only one other guy sitting on the side. Only twelve guys showed. At Carver half the school would have been trying out. The guy sitting on the side was about six feet and built pretty nice but he didn't look hard enough to play no ball. If only twelve guys showed up we'd probably all be on the team.

I watched the guys run. A couple of them had some game, most of them weren't that much. Ducky, the first guy I had met at Latimer, was on the court looking like he was hoping nobody would throw him the ball. Ducky's about five feet six, got red hair that's always hanging in his face, and this look on his face like maybe something hurts him. He couldn't even run right, let alone play no ball. But he was diving on the ball when it was on the floor and jumping for rebounds even when he didn't get close.

They didn't have many bloods at Latimer. The first day I got there and saw that Mr. Tate, the principal, was black, I thought most of the school was going to be black like Carver was. Hey, big time wrong. There was one brother on the floor, Jimmy Ellis. He was in some of my classes. He was okay, nothing great, but okay.

One of the white guys looked like he knew the game. I didn't know him. He moved nice and knew how to handle the ball. But then he wasn't going up against nothing great.

They played for a while and then the coach put in the other guy who was sitting on the side. He must have sent his rep down before him because everybody was backing off the dude and letting him run his show like he wanted it. He was the best thing on the court and everybody was treating him like he was.

"You," the coach pointed to me. "Take your shirt off and go in at center with the skins."

"I don't play center," I said. "I'm a guard."

"Then you just sit there," he said. He looked back at the game.

They ran the whole practice and I sat there. I guess I was supposed to run over and say I was going to go in at center. But center ain't my game, I'm a guard. I play facing the hoop and either dishing off or busting a move for the basket. Play me weak and I will definitely throw it down on you. Slam! That's my game, and it's sweet. When you love something, either a game or playing a horn or whatever it is you do, after a while you know what it's about. And what my game is about is something serious.

So the tryouts are over and the coach calls everybody over except me, checks off their names on his clipboard, and tells them they're on the team. I wasn't even worried because the dude hasn't seen me play. Mr. Goldstein asks him about me and I hear him saying something about not needing any prima donnas on the team.

"He probably can't play, anyway." He said that loud enough to make sure I heard him.

"Play better than anybody you got here," I said, loud enough for him to hear me.

He stands there for a while just looking at me and then he drops his clipboard to the floor like that's supposed to impress somebody.

"Get me a ball," he said to one of the kids on the bench. "Come on, hotshot, let's see what you got."

Now he's going to go one-on-one with me so he can diss me. Hey, I know the program. He's supposed to run his show and everybody is supposed to fall out because he got a game.

"Five baskets win," he says, and drops the ball on the floor so I got to pick it up. No problemo.

I took the ball out and he comes and starts leaning on me like old dudes do when they're too slow to keep up with you. I make a little fake and he's got his hands all over me.

"C'mon, I thought you were a guard."

I make the same little move and he puts his hands on me again. Then I fake the move and make another fake in the other direction and he goes for it. I put up a jump shot and it didn't touch anything but net. Made me feel good.

He takes the ball out and he's shaking his shoulders and nodding his head like I'm supposed to be nervous. He fakes, then goes up for a shot.

Hey, I'm seventeen years old, six feet four, a hundred and sixty-two pounds, and I can definitely rise. I go up and slap his mess away. I don't even chase the ball, I just put my hand on my hip and give him a look.

"My ball," he says. "You too lazy to get it before it goes out of bounds?"

"Your ball," I said, "my game."

I knew that was going to tick him off but he was out to diss me and it wasn't going to happen. Not in this life.

He tried to muscle past me, leaning all in on me and using his elbows. But I could hear his breathing and it was getting heavy. Sometimes when I play against old dudes in the hood they start laying on me and I know I just got to hold them off until they run out of breath, and then they got to throw up a prayer because they too tired to bust anything real.

He's pushing me and pushing me and then he starts looking to see where he is. For a while I'm holding him out, but I don't try nothing, just let him back me to the hoop. Then I ease off for a minute and he thinks he can turn. When he does I slap the ball away again.

This time I get it and when he comes to me I know what I got. I got a tired dude who can't get up. I put the ball on the floor one time hard, take a big step outside his left foot, shoot past him, and go up like I mean it.

I wasn't sure if I was getting up right but when I see the rim I know I'm not only right but righteous. I slammed it down as hard as I could.

The guys watching the game started yelling and carrying on and when I looked at the coach I saw that he was red. I should have just played it cool but instead I gave him a look which told him that I didn't respect his game.

"Nice move," he said. "What's your name?"

"Harris," I said. "Greg Harris, but you can call me Slam."

He didn't pick the ball up. He just told everybody to report to the gym for practice the next day.

Everybody was around me after the practice and telling me what a nice game I had. Everybody except the guy I thought could play. He dressed by himself in a corner. He looked a little freaky, or maybe it was the coat he wore. It was black and long, almost down to his ankles, like the old cowboy coats you see in the movies sometimes. When he left, he didn't say good-bye to anybody, just picked up his book bag and his horn and went.

"You and Nick are the best players on the team," Ducky said, outside the school.

"Who's Nick?" I asked.

"He's the guy with the long coat," Ducky said. "He plays bass sax. He's good, too."

I got home and told Derek I had made the basketball team.

"Grandma's sick," he said.

"What's wrong with her?"

"She's sick," he said. "I just told you that."

"You eat anything?"

"No, Moms left some money to get some cold cuts but they had a drive-by on 141st Street so I didn't go out," he said.

"Anybody get hurt?"

"A little girl got nicked," he said. "She ain't hurt bad."

Drive-bys really got to me. You can just be walking with somebody or going to the store and get shot because some dude don't know how to shoot straight. I didn't want to get shot on purpose, I knew I didn't want to get shot by accident.

CHAPTER TWO

My locker is right next to Ducky's and he thinks we're tight. We're not really tight but he's okay and he can play a whole mess of guitar. One time he showed me the callouses on his hands. He's real serious. But everything's like desperation time with him.

"Did you see the article in the paper?" he asked me.

"What article?"

Ducky pulls out a folded-up paper from his notebook and shows it to me.

DOING IT THE HARD WAY

Latimer Arts Magnet School is facing its fifth losing season in as many years. But the

South Bronx dancers, violinists, painters, and flute players will probably have the highest-average college enrollment in the city. They have their heads in the right places, the books, a rarity for high school students these days. But as for basketball, the Panthers will be doing a lot more purring than snarling.

"They got five losing seasons in a row?" I asked.

"Yeah, but they didn't have to write it up so we look like a bunch of wimps," Ducky said. "Especially that bit about us purring. You know what they're calling us?"

"Yeah, I went to Carver last year, remember?" I said. "When Carver played Latimer, the coach gave the game to the bench."

"You played for Carver?"

"I hurt my ankle so I didn't play much," I said. "And they had two good guards anyway. My friend Ice and a guy named Joe Crayton. Joe went on to play ball in junior college. If I had stayed at Carver, I would have taken his place this year."

"I bet we have a winning season this year," Ducky said.

"Bet on it," I said. I got my stuff from my locker and started on out the building.

Latimer is a magnet school, which means that kids from all over the city can come to it. They come by train mostly, but some that live in Manhattan can get a bus up to the Bronx. A few kids even come in from Mount Vernon and Yonkers. They're not supposed to be in the program but if they got an aunt or cousin or someone in the city they use their address. The school has a nice rep as a school for smart kids, mostly smart white kids.

I like the art lessons because you learn a lot. The dude who teaches art history is cool. He's tall, about my height and from some of the paintings he showed us he did when he was young he can definitely draw. Now he's just teaching. But when he shows you a painting he can make you see things in it that you wouldn't notice if you just looked at it yourself. And the things he likes, a line or the way the light hits something, are different. I'm not sure exactly why I like it when he's pleased about something, but I am. Most of the other classes were hard for me. When you have a lot of hard classes, one after the other, getting out of school at the end of the day is like getting out of a torture chamber or something. The streets in the South Bronx can look raggedy, but a day of classes when everybody knows what's going on but you can make them look good.

It was cold and the wind was picking up newspapers from the street and blowing them around as I walked crosstown. News from three days before was flapping through the streets like it didn't know it was old, like it was trying to be news again. The downtown train was crowded, mostly with kids from Roosevelt High. Some really fly Puerto Rican chicks were scoping me out and I gave them a look. I tried to remember what each one looked like so if I ever found one by herself I could say something like "Hey, don't you go to Roosevelt?" When the fly girls got off on 161st Street, I shot them a smile and one of them winked. I should have said something to them while they were on the train.

It was warm out for the first of December and a lot of people were out on their stoops when I reached the neighborhood. The lottery was up to twenty-something million dollars and people were running their mouths about that. Billy Giles, the guy who runs the bike shop, was showing off this new bike he had. He was saying that it only weighed fifteen pounds and had everybody lift it to check it out. It was light, but I don't like no light bicycle like that. It might be fast but if a car hit you on that light sucker you will definitely get a tag for your big toe.

Over in the park some guys were playing dominoes and having a good time. There was a girl there trying to sell some old jazz records but nobody was buying. She looked like a crack head and most of the dudes hated it when a girl got her string cut loose from crack. That's cause they know what she got to do to get the money for the stuff.

Some guys were running a full-court game but there was too much arguing and cursing going on. It was one of those games when they play two minutes and then argue five. They even argue about the score when they know what the score is.

The block was jumping. A guy was selling movie tapes near the subway stop. An old dude with one eye was selling sausages from a pushcart. Halfway down the street the car wash was busy because the weather had broke a little and the brothers were lined up to get their machines clean. With Christmas coming up everybody was trying to get some money together.

"Yo, Slam, what's happening!"

I turn and there's Ice walking down the street with Mtisha. Mtisha was looking her usual fine self.

"Man, what you doing walking down the street with my dream?" I asked Ice.

"How she your dream when we in love?" Ice comes back.

"Where y'all going?"

"To get some wedgies," Mtisha said. "Come on and go with us."

"I can't," I said. "You hurt my feelings walking down the street with Ice and deliberately looking as sweet as you can look."

"I knew I might meet you out here," Mtisha said. "Isn't that enough reason for me to start looking sweet?"

She came over to me and gave me some sugar and I put my arm around her. We started for the wedgies place just as this guy comes up with a shopping bag full of plastic statues.

"Hey, check it out," he said. He had on a dirty leather jacket and some greasy butt pants. "I got Malcolm, Martin Luther King, Jesus, and Muhammad Ali."

"Let's see Malcolm," Mtisha said, knowing she wasn't going to buy no statue.

"You got it." The brother goes through his bag and pulls out this little white statue that don't look nothing like Malcolm, and Mtisha gives me a look.

"That statue's white," Mtisha said.

"You got to paint the things, man," the brother said. "I'm letting them go for a dollar apiece. I was selling them yesterday for a pound."

"Let's see Martin Luther King," Mtisha said.

The brother went back into his bag and pulled out another statue. This one looked just like the first one and we all goofed behind it and went on into the wedgies joint. Mtisha ordered a large wedgies and a soda and asked me if I wanted anything.

"No, I'm good," I said.

"So how you like playing ball with them white boys up at Latimer?" Ice asked.

"They're okay," I answered.

"No they're not," Mtisha turned away from the counter. "Last year Carver beat them something pitiful."

"If you were back in Carver we'd be crushing people," Ice said. "They'd be calling us the Bruise Brothers!"

"I hear you," I said.

Ice and me used to go around saying we were brothers. That's the way I always felt about him, like he was my big brother and could do just about anything. He could hoop, he could dance, and he could get down with his hands if anybody messed with us.

"So when you coming back?" he asked.

"I got to stick with this," I said. "How's your moms?"

"Her jump shot is okay," Ice said. "But she ain't got your first step to the hoop."

"Get out of here, man." I took a handful of the potato wedgies from the bag that Mtisha offered me.

"You people going to block up the whole place?" the manager called over to us. "All you bought was the wedgies, you didn't pay no rent here."

"I'm putting your name on my list," Mtisha called to the manager. "And when the revolution comes I'm coming to get you personally."

"Yeah, well it ain't here yet so just get your fresh butt on out of here!"

It felt good to be with Ice and Mtisha. Ice and me used to live on St. Nicholas Avenue. We were always tight. When we were little our mothers used to have the same baby-sitter and every morning we used to have to eat oatmeal and then go to the potty together. If I couldn't make anything he would give me some of his so the baby-sitter would let us get up and play. I dug playing ball with him. It wasn't just his game, either. It was more the way we knew each other, the way we could be hanging on a corner and almost know what each other was thinking. We didn't talk about what we had, but it was there. A friend thing, almost like a love thing. The only time it really came out, or almost came out, was when we were on the court together. My last year at Carver things got a little cool for us. I figured maybe it was because Mtisha was crowding in on my mind, or maybe just that me and Ice were getting older and being close was harder than before. I don't know, but it seemed that Ice was getting harder. That's the way I figured things had to be. You live in the hood and either you get hard or you get wasted.

"So what you been doing with yourself?" I asked.

"Hanging loose," Ice said. "I got to get down to One-Two-Five Street and check out some beepers."

"Go on with your bad self," Mtisha said. She had a touch of ketchup on her face.

A lot of dudes were carrying beepers. It was like a big thing to show people you were into something. You couldn't bring a beeper into Carver because the principal there knew that the drug dealers used them. That's why kids liked them, pretending they were down with the rock trade. I didn't think it meant nothing that Ice was looking for one.

Ice gave Mtisha a peck on the cheek and went on to the subway. Mtisha and me started walking on down the block toward where I lived.

Ice and me were like really deep, deeper than me and Mtisha, but Mtisha was something else. I mean, if you were looking for something special, you found it when you ran up on that girl. She was deep brown, with dark eyes that just sparkled out at you. When she smiled at me it was like she meant that smile just for me personally and anybody else who saw it wouldn't even understand what was happening.

She kept telling me that she liked me but I shouldn't fall in love with her. What she needed to do was to tell my heart to stop doing its little dance when she came around and get her voice out my ear when I went to sleep at night. But in a way I knew what she meant about me not falling in love with her, because I knew she was going to college. Her father had gone to college and she was all set to go. It was like a thing with her, picking out what college she wanted to go to and seeing how they did in football games like that. That was a challenge to me, if I could deal with some girl that was going to college.

Thinking about that, about her going to college and about what Mr. Tate was saying about my grades and everything, was part of who I was. That was strange because it wasn't something I could touch or lay out so somebody else would know what it was I was feeling. In a way it was like a bad thing that was in my past and still with me, a memory of something that never happened.

"So you coming upstairs and saying hello to your future mother-in-law?" I asked, getting my mind on Mtisha.

"I got to sudy," Mtisha said. "I just needed a wedgies fix before I hit the books."

"Why don't you duck into the hall and throw some lips on me so I can feel good the rest of the day?"

"You ever think about coming back to Carver?" she asked.

We had reached my stoop and the usual dudes were there. One of them had a bottle in a brown paper bag. I took Mtisha by the arm and led her past them into the hallway.

"Come on upstairs for a while," I said.

"Slam, ain't no use in you getting yourself excited," Mtisha said. "All you getting from me is the wedgies."

"I can't even get a light kiss?"

"You ever think about coming back to Carver?" she asked again.

"I thought you wanted me to go to Latimer?"

"Yeah, I did," she said, leaning against the wall. Mrs. Ewing came out of her apartment, looked to see who I was with, then smiled when she saw it was Mtisha.

When Mrs. Ewing had left, Mtisha put her hand on my shoulder and I tried to sneak a kiss. I got her on the cheek.

"You know, Ice is messing around with the wrong dudes," she said.

"What you mean?"

"All of a sudden he got a lot of money," Mtisha went on. "Some people are saying that some of the scouts who come from colleges are giving him money. But some other folks are saying that they saw him hanging with some serious dealers over near Garvey Park."

"No way. Ice is my homey," I said. "And he's a senior. Maybe those college scouts are giving him money."

"They lay any money on you?" Mtisha said. "You're as good as Ice."

"I'm not a senior," I said. "And they're not coming to Latimer looking for ballplayers."

"I wish you were back at Carver so you could check him out."

"You got a thing for Ice?"

"A *thing*?" Mtisha pushed away from me. "How long has Ice been our friend?"

"Forever," I said.

"Tell me about it!" Mtisha was serious. "I think you need to drop that brother a very heavy dime."

"Suppose you're wrong?" I said. "Then I'm dissing him for nothing."

"If you can't watch your brother's back without dissing him, then you need to seriously check out your relationship," Mtisha said.

"Are you watching my back?"

"Uh-uh, because that ain't where you're dangerous, sweetie pie," she said, smiling.

She put her face to mine, pushed me just a little off balance, then darted her tongue into my mouth. By the time I got my balance and was ready for some heavy action she was wagging her finger at me and going out the door. My heart was sending out some serious love signals to that girl.

On the way upstairs I thought about what she

had said about Ice. His real name was Benny Reese but everybody called him Ice because he looked like Ice T, the old rapper. As long as I had known him he was hip to the whole drug scene. There wasn't any way you couldn't be and live where we lived. We've stepped over the bodies in the hallways, seen strong guys turn weak and cops spread sheets over brothers in the gutter.

What else we knew was basketball. We'd play all summer, sweating from morning to late afternoon, and in the winter we'd shovel the snow away in the park so we could still play. We had the neighborhood and basketball and each other and those were the truths we had. Everything else was a maybe or a could be.

I couldn't figure Ice to be standing on some corner dealing. We had seen too many guys get messed up. When you dealt, the police could bust you any time they wanted to. They knew who was dealing and who wasn't. One day you would see a guy on the corner being slick and the next day you would hear he was hooked up in a cell somewhere.

Not only that, but Ice had one of the sweetest games in the city. Mtisha said I was as good as he was and it was close, but I had to give him his respect and say that his game was about as close to all-world as you could get. Everybody was looking at him like they were waiting for him to hit the NBA. I knew he wasn't giving all that up to deal on no corner.

I got into the house and Moms was dressed. She said she was going to the hospital to see Grandma and I could go with her now or the next day.

"I'll check it out tomorrow," I said.

My room seemed smaller than it usually was, like it was closing in on me. I turned on the radio and spun the dial looking for some decent jams. For a while I just lay on the bed, checking out how the cracks in the ceiling looked like a map. I tried to follow one of the cracks to see if I could make it into a corner. Then I got up and went out to the kitchen to see if Moms had left for the hospital. She was gone so I went back to my room. I turned the radio up higher.

What I didn't want to think about was Ice messing with no crack. Scenes with him in it kept popping into my head. One time over the summer I saw him sitting on the park bench in Garvey Park. He was with some dudes I didn't know and drinking from a bag and said it was a forty but his eyes didn't look right to me, they looked glassy and had that far away feel you get from heads. I had let it ride, laying off some lame excuse like I had to get uptown even though I was carrying my ball. I remember walking away to the other side of the park and then turning back and looking through the fence to where he was. What I felt at the time was scared for him. Then I told myself he was just dealing with the forty and I'd call him on it later. Beer would slow his game down.

But if Mtisha was peeping something strange about Ice I knew I should check it out. I knew it and didn't want to do it. I was scared again.

CHAPTER THREE

I don't like hospitals. Whenever I think of hospitals all I can think of is people dying and stuff like that. I've never been sick a day in my life. I don't even catch colds.

"I know you're not wearing those raggedy sneakers to the hospital," Moms said. "Your grandmother's not in a coma, you know."

"These sneakers ain't raggedy," I said.

"Those sneakers *aren't* raggedy," she said. "And yes they are too raggedy to be going to the hospital to see your grandmother."

Right. So we get dressed and walk on down to 135th Street where Harlem Hospital is. We had to go in past the guards and the downstairs desk. They gave us two blue passes and told us to go to the fourth floor.

We get up there by elevator and a nurse, kind of fine-looking, tells us where to go.

Grandma had another person in her room, a woman who looked like she was really tore down. She was light-skinned and skinny with white hair and she was breathing funny. When we got to the room the woman pulled a curtain around her bed. I was glad because I didn't want to see her.

"How you doing, Mama?" That's what my mother said to her mother, which was cool.

"I'd be doing a lot better if whoever it is they got fixing the food here knew how to cook!" Grandma Ellie said. "All they know how to fix here is watery mashed potatoes and something so bad Hamburger Helper done give up on it."

"You know the doctor doesn't want you to eat any fatty foods," Mama said. "He told you that, didn't he?"

"Before they let a doctor tell people what they can eat and what they can't eat they should find out how good his mama cooks," Grandma Ellie said. "If his mama can't cook then he don't know what good food is and he don't care what he give you."

"I told Greg he didn't have to come but he insisted on seeing his grandmother," Mama lied.

"Why on earth do you want to be in a hospital

on a nice day like this?" Grandma Ellie asked me. "You ain't got no friends? Maybe it's your breath."

"Get out of here, Grandma." I sat on the edge of the bed and saw Moms make a face. "I just wanted to check you out."

"I'm doing okay." Grandma Ellie looked away from us toward the window. "You know, when you reach my age things don't work like they supposed to. You liable to wake up in the morning and have an arm fall off, or maybe one leg don't want to walk right."

"Did the doctor get the results back?" Moms asked.

"Yeah. He said a whole lot of things which all added up to the fact that I was sick. Well, I could have told the young fool that from the start."

"He say what was wrong?"

"Said I'm old, and I'm creaky, and that old creaky people don't get around like young juicy people," Grandma Ellie said. "But the doctor talked about me, and the nurse talked about me, and I'm tired of hearing about how sick I am, and how many pills I got to be taking and all. Tell me what you people are doing."

"Just making it from day to day," Mama said. "Trying to get Greg to get his head into the books."

"What's wrong with you and them books, boy?" Grandma Ellie's voice flattened.

"Nothing wrong with them," I said. "Just I'm in a new school and the other kids had more math than me."

"That's the only subject you having trouble in?"

"I'm a little bit behind in everything, I guess," I said. "The school I'm in is more advanced than my old school."

"It's hard, ain't it, son?" Grandma Ellie put her hand on my shoulder.

"Yes, ma'am."

"Well, I just want to share this with you, baby," she said, softly. "I really don't care because it's not my life. And I'd bet two Roosevelt dimes that nobody else cares — maybe excepting your mama and that's cause she still thinks it's her job — because it ain't their lives. It's your life, do you care?"

"Yeah."

"Then deal with it."

"Yes, ma'am."

I didn't appreciate Grandma Ellie running me down like that. It's not that I didn't want to give her respect, but I don't think she should have run it down on me like she did.

"He got a new assignment," Moms said. "He's

supposed to explore his environment. That's where he lives and everywhere."

"I know what environment means, Mavis," Grandma Ellie said. "You going to do one of those television programs on our neighborhood?"

"No."

"Lord, don't tell me you got your lip stuck out because I told you I don't care about how you doing in school?"

I didn't have nothing to say because I thought she was just running me down because she could. I put my mind on something else completely. She and Moms ran their mouths for a while more and then it was time to leave. Moms kissed Grandma Ellie and I kissed her and we were ready to leave and peace out but Grandma Ellie couldn't leave it alone.

"When you finish your television program I'd like to see it," she said.

Yeah. Sure.

We did the kissing thing again and then we left. Moms said she was coming back in the evening and said that Derek wanted to come, too.

In the elevator on the way down a guy with a bandaged face was moaning real loud and the woman with him was patting him on the shoulder. The guy must have been about fifty years old and acting like a baby. I was looking at this and I didn't even notice Moms crying until we got into the lobby.

It didn't take no whole lot to figure she was crying cause her mother was sick, but I asked her anyway.

"Just the idea of losing her shakes me up," she said. "It's the kind of thing you don't want to talk about."

"What she got?"

"She had a tumor, but now it's spread," she said. She teared up again and turned away. Hey, I don't like to see her cry. I don't like to see her cry for no reason. But like when it's about somebody being sick and stuff it's even worse.

We went on home and Pops had made some supper. We had black beans and oxtails and collard greens and rice. It was good. I can get into some oxtails.

CHAPTER FOUR

We had two practices during the week and they were both bad. The coach had this thing where every play was going to come off a pattern. The guards were supposed to bring the ball down center court, then signal the pattern and everybody was supposed to run it. That way everybody was supposed to know what everybody else was doing. The guards were Trip, Nick Young, me, and Ducky. Ducky was a guard because he was too small to be anything else, not because he could play. He couldn't dribble without looking at the ball, which was his main problem.

Anyway, during the first practice the coach kept us running patterns that were supposed to end in an easy layup for one of the forwards. But what happened was that the picks didn't work, or if they did it was just because everybody knew what the play was supposed to be and stopped when they saw the pick. Half the time they would have to pass the ball back out to the guards and we'd end up running the same play over again.

We ended the practice with everyone shooting from the three-point line. A lot of the guys, even Ducky, could shoot threes when nobody was on them. It wasn't a sweat practice. I figured maybe the practices would get better later on.

When I got back to the block, some kids had set up a hoop in front of the bicycle shop and were playing some rough three-on-three. Derek was playing and I watched him. He looked pretty good until he saw me watching him, then he tried to showboat. I went upstairs and he came up a little later, smelling from the sweat and with his pants split up the back.

"They ain't your school pants, right?" I asked.

"You going to sew them up for me?" he asked. "I'll give you two dollars to sew them up before Mom gets home," he said.

"Where'd you get two dollars from?"

"Daddy."

"He was drinking?"

"No, he just gave me the two dollars," Derek said.

I got the needle and thread from Moms' room and started sewing up Derek's pants. He had just split the seam so it wasn't any big deal.

"How I look out there?" he asked. "Pretty good, huh?"

"Not as good as me," I said.

"I'm not as old as you are," he said. "Could I make your school team?"

"What position you going to play?" I asked.

"I'll be the guy that shoots the ball."

"That's my job, and you can't make it," I said. "Plus we got two other guards that can play. Both of them are around six feet."

"I'll make it when I go to Latimer," Derek said.

"You going to Latimer?"

"That's where all the brainiacs go, isn't it?"

"Are you a brainiac?"

"Yep," he shook his head like he meant it, too.

"Get on with your bad self."

I finished his pants, got the two dollars, and gave him one back. He went on a fridge raid and I took out my books and started looking over my homework. I wondered if Derek thought I was a brainiac because I went to Latimer. I knew I didn't think I was one.

We had the second practice on a Monday at lunchtime and the coach divided us up into a

"Red" team and a "Blue" team. Trip and Nick were the guards on the Red team and me and Ducky were the guards on the Blue team. Trip and Nick took turns picking me and driving past Ducky. But they weren't making legitimate picks. They were stepping out and blocking me so I couldn't get past. But when I got the ball and put a move on Trip, the coach got on my case.

"You have any idea of what team ball is supposed to be?" he asked me.

"Yeah."

"Are you bright enough to remember that we're supposed to be *playing* team ball?"

"What's it got to do with being bright?" I asked.

"Then why don't you tell me what it *has* got to do with?" he said.

I walked off the court. Later for that fool. He was giving everybody else their propers, but he wasn't showing me nothing. Even if he had a beef he didn't have to diss me right there on the floor.

Mr. Goldstein came into the locker room a little after I got in there. I was changing clothes and he sat down on the rubbing table and asked me what was wrong.

"You didn't see what was going on out there?" I asked him.

"I saw what was going on but I might interpret it differently than you did," Mr. Goldstein said. "He needs you to concentrate on playing the kind of pattern ball that he thinks is going to help the team win. What's wrong with that?"

"How come Nick and Trip don't have to do it the same way I do?" I said.

"Because he wants to give the starters more latitude," Mr. Goldstein said. "They have to run the game."

"What you know about basketball?"

"I used to coach the team here," he said. "Then I had a heart attack and had to give it up. I work part time now. But I know the game. I know the game and I know what you got in here."

He reached over and tapped my chest.

Goldy, that's what everybody called him, was thin, a little stooped, with a long face that always looked a little down. He didn't have much hair, just a few white strands that he combed across the top of his head.

"You used to play?" I asked.

"A little. I was never that good. If they played like they do today I would never have made a team. I enjoyed the game, though. Like you do. It was important to me."

"Why?"

"It was something I could do," Goldy said. "I might not have been great, but I was better than most kids in my neighborhood."

He talked some other stuff but I wasn't even listening. I was thinking about Nick and Trip starting and me being on the bench. It was like I was some kind of a scrub or something.

"Take a shower," Goldy was saying, "and try to calm down. And when you start feeling sorry for yourself and thinking that life isn't fair, ask yourself is it fair for you to have so much talent and some of the other kids not to have it?"

"Yeah."

In the afternoon this white girl named Karen slipped me a note in English. It said "Will you pose for me tomorrow after school?" I wasn't too sure what she meant by that. Why did she want to draw me? Then I figured maybe she was hitting on me. She had a nice face and a real tough body so I figured maybe I would give her a play. The more I thought about it the more I figured she must have been checking me out and decided that she liked what she saw. She was probably kind of shy so she had to slip me the note instead of dealing with it face-to-face. That was all good because I liked shy girls. And it was okay that she was white, too. I'm not prejudiced or anything like that.

What I was hoping was that she didn't want to jump into any heavy stuff too fast. You got to worry about things like safe sex and girls getting pregnant before they get married. The thing was that if we messed around and she did get pregnant I would probably have to have some help supporting her until I got to the NBA. I'd have to explain all that to her folks because they might be prejudiced.

Once I got to the NBA and started pulling down those big bucks we could get a house in the country or maybe in California. Actually, it would probably depend on who I was playing for. If I was playing for the Knicks I'd get an apartment in Manhattan, across from Central Park. One of those fancy apartments with about three or four bedrooms in case we had more kids.

The English teacher said we had to turn in a term paper or a photo essay on somebody we admired. Then the period ended and Karen came right over to me.

"You going to pose?" she asked.

"Yeah," I said. "I'll give it a shot."

"Okay, here's the picture I want." She laid a picture on my desk and gives me this little smile. "We'll meet in the band room at three-thirty. See you later."

Then she was gone.

I looked at the picture. All it was were a pair of old-looking hands looking like they were praying. Under it was written "Durer." The dude could definitely draw.

I went on home thinking about the picture and Karen. The more I thought about her the more I was against marrying her in the first place.

Derek was home when I got there and he asked me what I thought about Grandma being sick.

"What you mean?"

"She looked all right to me," Derek said.

"She's sick on the inside," I said. "Not on the outside. Were you just born stupid or something?"

"I just asked you a question," he said. "You don't have to jump bad, man."

"Yeah, right."

I went on into my bedroom and opened my math book again. I thought I was studying but after a while I saw that I was just looking at the book but not thinking about the math. What I was thinking about was Mr. Nipper and the basketball practice.

The thing was that everybody had to be about something, and I was about ball. He didn't have to diss me on the ball court. That was wrong and he knew it was wrong but he didn't care. Where that put me was I had to either quit and give up what I was about or go back and still play with the team and just give up my respect.

The picture that Karen gave me was on the bed and I looked at it and put my hands like the guy had it in the picture. I looked in the mirror and it looked whack. I tried to relax my shoulders and do it again but it was still looking stupid so I put it back in my binder.

The remote was on the end table and I grabbed it. The dancers on the screen moved to a steady beat. The music reached for my mind and I let it go.

CHAPTER FIVE

So it's Friday morning and I'm sitting in history listening to Mr. Penny, the history teacher, talk about all the arguments they had before they set up the Constitution. It was boring because I didn't see what difference it made. Mr. Penny caught this kid named Joe Ming reading the paper under his desk and asked him what his problem was.

"Isn't it the Constitution that's important?" Joe asked. "Not what they said on the way to drafting it?"

"But if you're looking for clues to what they meant when they wrote certain parts of the Constitution it helps to know what the arguments were leading up to the writing."

Mr. Penny liked talking to Joe and you could tell. Everybody else in the class liked him talking to Joe, too, because he wouldn't mess with us. I let my mind drift off to when I was supposed to pose for Karen. Karen had probably saw my hands in class and knew they were like classical hands or something. I liked getting into things with other kids in the school. That was a difference between Latimer and Carver. At Latimer the kids were always looking to get into something.

Karen was in the band room and so was Charley Movalli, and some other kids. They were just hanging out but when Karen started setting up her drawing pad they came over to check us out. She said she was ready and I got my hands in the pose.

Karen started sketching. She threw the first one away after a bit and started a second one right away.

In about two minutes there was a whole stream of people walking in, checking out my hands and Karen's sketch. I really wasn't going for it too tough but I kept trying to keep my hands still.

"Say, Slam, why do you have your face fixed like that," Charley asked. "She's only drawing your hands."

"I got to be in the mood," I said, trying to feel holy.

After she finished I checked out her drawing. It was good. I could draw but she was really doing it.

On the way out of school she told me I had great hands.

I might marry her after all.

In the morning a boy came into the room and gave Mr. Aumack, my homeroom teacher, a note. Aumack read it, and then called me to the front of the room.

"Go to the office," he said.

I went out of the room with the kid from the office.

"What's up?" I asked him.

"Your parents are in Mr. Tate's office," he said.

I thought something had happened to Derek. Maybe he got hit by a car or something. Then I thought that maybe Grandma had died. I ran down the stairs two at a time and got to the office as soon as I could.

I went through the reception area and right into Mr. Tate's office. My moms was sitting there with a black guy, but it wasn't my father. He looked like somebody who worked in an office. Moms wasn't crying or anything so I figured nobody had died.

"Greg, I'd like you to meet Richie Randall," Mr. Tate said. "I've known Richie for a long time. He's a graduate of Howard University, and a working engineer. He's also with the Guardians.

"The Guardians volunteer some of their time to tutor and counsel young African Americans. I've talked it over with Richie, and with your mother, and we think that you can benefit quite a bit by having Richie tutor you in math."

"I understand they call you Slam," this guy says to me.

"Yeah?"

"Well, Slam, I would like to work with you to get your math grades up," the guy said. "You think we can work together?"

"No, man," I said.

"Mr. Tate doesn't think you can continue playing ball if you don't get your grades up," Moms said.

"I don't need nobody working with me," I said. "Nothing wrong with me."

"That's not the point," Mr. Tate said. "The point is you need to improve your grades, pure and simple. If you expect a decent life — nice family, house, car, couple of kids — then you have to get a good foundation. And here's where you start. Right here in Latimer."

"I'll think about it," I said.

"That's a good idea," the engineer dude said. "Maybe we can get together some time and have a soda."

The bell rang and I could hear the kids changing classes in the hall. I didn't want to be standing in the office, and I didn't want this guy looking at me, and I didn't want to even look at my moms.

"You better think hard, son," Mr. Tate said.

"You ain't my father, so don't be calling me 'son,'" I said. Then I walked out of the office and went outside and sat on the steps. It was cold but I didn't care.

Like what was I supposed to be, stupid or something? Mr. Tate talking all that mess about how my life is going to get messed up and about what kind of family I'm going to have. What did he know about what kind of family I was going to have?

I didn't need people talking about me like I was some kind of thing they was studying in science. A thing, and not even a person. They were talking about me like I was nothing. Ain't nobody wants to be nobody. Mess just made me feel like hitting something.

Then my moms is coming out the door and she sees me sitting there and she comes over and puts her arm around me.

"Mr. Tate just wanted you to meet Mr. Randall before you and me talked about him," she said. "He looks like a nice guy."

"What did Pops say?"

"We haven't talked about it yet," she said. "But I think he'll see that it's for your good. He'll go along with it, honey. Will you at least give it a chance?"

"I'll think about it," I said.

The thing was that anytime somebody was talking to me they was telling me what I was doing wrong. Hearing how you're wrong all the time gets old in a hurry. Everybody telling me how they talking to me for my own good. Yeah, all that's good. But if I can't fly don't be taking me to your cloud.

Pops was laid off again and sitting around the house a lot. Ed's Auto Electric Shop was starting a cab business and was looking for drivers but you had to pay your own insurance and we didn't have the money for that. I asked Moms if she had talked to Pops about the guy we had met in school. She shook her head.

"You can't even tell him that you bringing in another dude to take his place," I said. "How you think I feel about it?"

"I'm not bringing in another *dude* to do *anything*!" she snapped back at me.

"Then what you doing?" I asked.

There wasn't any reason to wait for her answer. I knew what she was going to say, what she always said, that what she was doing was about making it in the real world, the world past Billy's bike shop and past Akbar's dog and past the small hills of garbage and dirty snow that would just end up as dirty water running down the streets nobody cared for.

Pops didn't really make a difference in the set. When it got time to get real he wasn't making it and she felt she had to get somebody else in, somebody who graduated from college and could talk like he knew people had to listen to him. It was about math and it wasn't about math. Because after we had dealt with the math there would be something else. All you had to do was to look around the hood. All the math in the world wasn't changing the hood.

Pop's brown skin was my brown skin. The way his hair grew was the way mine grew. He couldn't play no ball but there was something in the way he moved, something in the way he walked, that was me. I could feel it more than say it, but I knew it was true.

"Okay, let's set the big picture." Mr. Nipper had his foot up on a chair. He was wearing a suit and tie with sneakers. He looked okay. "Because of the budget problems in some of the schools we're going to have a short regular season this year and then go to the championship rounds. Maybe next year we can get back to the regular schedule. The way they're trying to make it fair is to make more divisions. There are eight teams in our division and I think we have a chance of doing well. Goldy, you have the list of schools?"

"Regis, St. Peter's, Trinity, Country Day, Hunter, Harlem School of the Arts, Carver, and us," Mr. Goldstein read off the list.

"Carver handled us pretty easily last year," Mr. Nipper said. "But they're in the league and we have to deal with them and everybody else. We'll play each team one time. At the end of the round-robin tournament the two teams with the best records will play each other for the division championship. The division champions will then play for the City P.S.A.L. championships. I'm going to try to schedule a couple of non-league games in, too. Just for the experience.

"So every game is going to be important. If we beat the best teams and lose to the worst we'll still be hurting our record. We have a pretty good squad and we can be there at the end if we play together as a team. We're down to ten players and I'm going to stick with the ten unless somebody gets hurt. That way everybody gets to play. Jimmy's going to be our starting center. Frank and Tony will be at the forwards and Nick and Trip will be the starting guards, but everybody on the team is important and everybody will get a chance to play."

I was still ticked off because I wasn't starting but I figured that once I got to play in a game things would turn around.

Our first game was at home against Regis and when we got out onto the floor they were already warming up. They had some size on us but it didn't look that bad. We ran our warm-up drills and then sat down to wait for the tip-off.

The Regis cheerleaders were looking like they just fell out from a magazine they looked so good. They had the same color outfits as the ballplayers and they all wore these big red-frame glasses with no glass in them.

Our cheerleaders had a few nice cheers but they weren't as sharp as the ones from Regis. Plus, the people who came to see Regis play had a big banner in the stands. They were looking good.

I thought I heard my name and looked up and saw about five guys from the hood, including Ice. He made a fist and held it up in the air and I held mine up. That just made me feel worse about not starting.

"I want everybody on the bench to stay alert and be ready to go in," Goldy said.

The game started and Regis got the opening tap. The guy that got the tap dribbled right past our whole team and made a layup. That happens sometimes when you first start a game so I didn't think nothing of it.

Trip brought the ball in to Nick and the Panthers had their first offensive play. Nick made a signal and everybody forgot everything they had been doing in practice. Guys were running all over the place and Nick was out there near the top of the key looking for somebody to get open. Finally, he passes the ball in to Jimmy and Jimmy turns and starts a little hook. The center from Regis went up and slapped Jimmy's shot away and the Regis fans were cheering.

Regis got the ball and came downcourt fast. They passed the ball to one of their forwards coming along the baseline and he passed it to their center. The center went up, made the deuce, and got the foul. Jimmy held his hand up because he had fouled the guy.

Their center made the foul shot and we were behind by five.

Regis was playing a zone but it didn't look that tough because they were just standing around. They kept their hands up but nobody on our team was really challenging their zone. That let them collapse under the basket and box out for the rebounds. We were getting one shot at a time and they weren't even the best shots. The coach put in Glen for Tony Fornay and he moved a little more than Tony did but not enough to change the game.

At the end of the first quarter the score was Regis 18 and Latimer 9. By the half the score was Regis 30 and Latimer 21.

The way it looked was like either school could win. Regis wasn't that good, but the only players on our team who were doing anything was Nick and Trip. Jimmy was standing around the paint so much he got called for two three-second violations, and our forwards looked like they were just throwing the ball toward the backboards and hoping for the best. I looked up at Ice and he just shook his head.

The coach gave a big speech about how we were still in the game and how he wanted every loose ball. We went back out to warm up for the second half and Ice came over to the side of the court and called me over.

"How come you ain't playing?" he asked.

"The coach don't like me or something," I said.

"Tell him I said you need to get some game," Ice said.

I know I needed to get some game. I had been looking forward to playing all day and now I was just sitting on the bench.

"Hey, Greg! Come here!" the coach called me over.

"What's that guy's name?" the coach asked me. "The guy you were talking to just now."

"Benny Reese," I said, using his real name.

"They call him Ice?"

"Yeah."

"That's who I thought it was," he said. Then he walked away.

Hey, that blew my mind. My coach had heard about Ice. Probably had even seen him before.

The first five minutes of the second half was real sloppy. We stunk and so did Regis but they got up by twelve points. Then, when one of their players got fouled, the coach took out both Glen and Frank, moved Jimmy over to forward, put Jose at center and put Trip at the other forward.

"Greg, get in."

At first I didn't even realize he was talking to me but then Ducky pushed my arm and I woke up. I went over to the scorer's table and reported in.

When I got on the court my homeys started whooping. It made me feel good.

"Yo! Slam! Slam! Slam!" That was from my man Ice.

There hadn't been one dunk in the whole game but I knew there was going to be one soon. I in-bounded the ball to Nick and he went down the center, threw a little head fake on his man, and ran him into a pick. He looked like he was in the clear but when he went up to take his shot their center, who was knocking everything down, pinned his stuff against the boards and then pulled it down.

On the way downcourt Nick gives me this funny look like he was embarrassed that the Regis center had thrown away his stuff.

"I'm going for the pill," I said. "Get him if he spins."

Their guard came down center court and I went after him when he got a foot from the mid-court line. He got over the line all right and spun just the way I thought he might. But Nick came up on his blind side when he saw the spin and knocked the ball away. Nick started downcourt and their whole team was after him.

I was busting tail downcourt when I saw Nick stop and hold up the play. Trip came out to him and got the ball for a hot minute and passed it right back to Nick. But both their forwards were outside with the guards and I got loose on the left side. Nick took a step to the right and threw a hard pass to me. I turned and saw their center moving toward me.

I put the ball on the floor for a quick beat and then took it to the metal. The pill was cupped between my fingers and my wrist, and I felt the move. It was like the whole thing was going down in slow motion and I was in it and watching it at the same time. Their center was going up, arching his back away from me so he wouldn't get a body foul, and getting his hands up as high as he could.

I saw his forehead and then I saw the rim and then I felt the pebble grain against my fingertips as I slammed the ball with everything I had. When my palm slapped against the rim it felt good. It felt good.

CHAPTER SIX

It was like we had just been out there toying with them before I slammed over their big man. Everybody got into the defense and we started doing some serious ball-hawking. Regis had two guys who could handle the ball pretty good and we had three guys, me, Trip, and Nick, who could go get it. We stole the ball twice and got them in a backcourt violation once. The result was six more points for us and their coach called a time-out. We were only down by four.

"See who they're bringing in." The coach pushed Goldy toward the scorer's table.

"How many fouls do I have?" Trip asked. He poured some water on one of the towels and put it on the back of his neck. You could see the excitement on the bench.

"Only two, you're cool."

"We don't want to give them foul shots," the coach said. "We have to make them work for everything they get."

"They're putting in one of their seniors." Goldy came back to the bench. "He's got to be a ballhandler."

"Okay, listen up, guys." The coach knelt down in front of us. "They're probably going to try to slow the game down and draw fouls. We've got nine minutes to play, that's plenty of time. What we need is board control. We can't let them get second and third shots. Let's go get them!"

We got back on the floor and they inbounded. The coach was right, the new Regis player could handle the ball and they were slowing things down, working the ball in and out, looking for the easy deuce.

My man wasn't doing squat, just running in circles like he was waiting for some dynamite pass, but I think he just didn't want the ball. I started playing him real loose and kept switching off on number 5, Trip's man. He saw me coming and got the pass off to my man at the top of the key, and I turned and ran back to my man. He tried to get rid of the ball back to number 5, but Trip picked it off.

We got downcourt with Trip on the point and

Nick cutting across the lane. They picked up Trip and he bounced the ball into me and I was one-on-one with their center again and I was deep. A fake got him up in the air and I was around him and laid it up for two.

From there on in it was like a practice session. We kept double-teaming the ball and they kept throwing it away. They had lost their nerve. We went up by six, and then by nine with a minute to go.

I wanted one more slam and I got it when Nick and Tony, who was back in the game in Jimmy's place, double-teamed one of their forwards. I could see he was spooked.

"Ball! Ball!" I called to him and he just let it go to me.

The guy who had lost the ball to me was the only one coming after me as I went downcourt. He was two steps behind when I hit the foul line, and when I took my takeoff step he was still on the wood. I went up turning and flying and threw it down on a bad reverse slam and I could hear everybody screaming.

They were still screaming as Regis went through the motions of walking the ball down and watching the clock tick the time off. Twenty seconds . . . ten seconds . . . five . . . and the buzzer went off. We had won by eleven points.

We shook hands with the Regis players and then went into the locker room. After the showers the coach talked to us about how we had hung in earlier and how well we had played on defense. He didn't say anything about me but I knew he had to be thinking.

"Yo, Slam, how many points did you have?" Ducky asked.

"I don't know, man," I answered him. "Check with the scorekeeper."

It turned out that I had eleven points, exactly the amount we beat Regis by. It also turned out that everybody on the team was calling me Slam, instead of Greg.

Nick grabbed me by the arm on the way out of the locker room.

"You got a tough game, man," he said.

"Yeah, thanks," I said.

I waved to the guys as I made my way through the kids leaving Latimer. A lot of kids waved to me or called out things. The guys from the team were walking together in twos and threes and I knew they were talking about the game, and about winning. There weren't a whole lot of times I had a chance to win anything.

Ice was waiting for me outside. He had two okay-looking girls with him. One was wearing a nose stud and three studs in her ear, all on the right side. She was wearing some tight pants that were the same color as her skin, a light sienna, and for a second I thought she didn't have any pants on.

"You lit them up good," Ice said. "What they doing, keeping you out for a half to keep the game close?"

"The coach is a trip," I said. "You know, he got his thing, and I got mine."

"We're going out to Laurelton," Ice said. "Come on and take a ride with us."

Moms expected me home but I didn't really want to go home right away. I was feeling high from the game and I knew if I went home I would have to go back to dealing with homework and school. So I told Ice I'd go with him.

The car was a tough-looking silver Benz. It had a leather interior and a wood dashboard. It was definitely on the money.

Ice and one girl, Bianca, sat in the front seat of the car and me and the other girl, the one with the tight pants, sat in the back. Her name was Ceil but she said everybody called her 'Kicky.' Hey, that was cool with me.

Kicky sat right next to me and, when Ice put his arm around Bianca, Kicky snuggled up to me and I put mine around her.

"You got strong," Ice said as we headed down toward the Triboro Bridge. "You used to get up but you didn't get up so smooth."

"I did some weight workouts over the summer," I said. "I was calling you."

"Yeah, yeah." I could see the outline of Ice's head in the dark car. "But I was running here and there over the summer, you know, trying to get paid."

"I hear that."

We started joking about Ice running for mayor of New York and me running for governor. Ice said we should go for the ex-convict vote.

"You got more people been in jail in New York than been in college," Bianca said. "I read that in the newspaper."

"You going to be a Republican or a Democrat?" Kicky asked.

"I'm running on the Salami Party ticket," Ice said. "That's just one step past the Baloney Party."

Ice stopped off to see a guy he knew off Merrick Boulevard. He just popped in for a minute and then popped out and then we stopped at a place to get some ice cream. It was cold but we still wanted it. We were sitting there when Ice asked me if I thought that Carver and Latimer were going to play for the championship.

"I don't know," I said. "You see any of the other teams play?"

"We played St. Peter's and just beat them," he said. "We would have killed them if the referees didn't call a foul every time you looked at one of them. We ain't played nobody yet that we couldn't mess over."

I didn't know if that sounded good for Latimer or not. Ice went on talking about this white boy who played for Trinity. He didn't look like he could play. He wore a pony tail in the back and had the sides of his head shaved. Ice said he looked like a freak but he could really hoop.

The waitress came over and asked if we wanted anything else and Bianca wanted another soda and Kicky asked if smoking was allowed.

"No, because the owner got asthma," the waitress said. "He used to smoke more than anybody before he got it, too."

"I'm going out in the car and grab a smoke," Kicky said. Then she turned to me. "You want to come out and wait with me?"

"Yeah, okay," I said.

"We'll wait for you out there," Kicky said. She started getting up.

"Yeah, okay." Ice grinned and tossed me the keys. "But don't be steaming up the windows."

I opened the door and we got into the backseat. I didn't like being around people smoking but I didn't mind it some of the time. Kicky lit up her cigarette and offered me one.

"No, I got to play ball," I said.

"I'm thinking of giving it up," she said. "But I'm afraid if I stop smoking I'll start gaining a lot of weight."

"Yeah, I hear what you saying."

"And my mother is like so heavy her whole life is going whack," Kicky said. She went through her bag and pulled out a portable tape player. "Who you like to listen to?"

"Whatever," I said. "I change up a lot."

"You like Seal?"

"He's okay," I answered.

"I think he's nasty-looking," she said, smiling.

"He looks all right to me," I said.

When she puffed on the cigarette the tip glowed in the dark. She blew out some smoke and gave me a smile and put the cigarette back in her mouth. Mtisha came into my mind. It would have been great if she had been in the car with me.

"If you didn't have that cigarette in your mouth I'd give you a big kiss," I said.

"Get out of here with that corny line," she said.

"You look like one of them shy guys anyway. You know, I hate shy boys."

"I'm not that shy," I said. I couldn't think of anything great to say so I tried to look cool, like I knew something. She just looked at me and smiled. She looked better when she was smiling and I threw her a smile back.

"Give me the keys," Kicky said.

She leaned over the front seat, fumbled with the radio and got it on. Somebody was singing something about 'Hold on my heart' or something like that.

"Why don't you crack the windows in front?" she said. "Then show me how not that shy you are?"

Something said to leave it alone, to go on back to where Ice and Bianca were. The problem was doing it without looking lame. I reached over and hit the button that rolled down the front window.

"So what you got to say for yourself?" Kicky scooted down in the seat. She was short and I figured she could have laid out on that backseat.

"Where did Ice get the car?" I asked her.

"I think it's his cousin's," she said. "You like this song?"

I didn't want to think about the car, so instead of answering Kicky I just leaned over and started kissing her. She was just lying back when I first kissed her but then she wrapped one of her legs around me and started tongue kissing me. She was something else. She didn't even know me but she was kissing me as if we had a thing going on and I thought I could have done anything to her that I wanted to. We must have kissed for about I don't even know how long before Ice and Bianca came to the car.

"I ought to charge you people rent," Ice said.

They kept the windows cracked and we drove around for about an hour more. It felt good sitting in the back of a nice machine with Kicky sitting in my lap kissing on me while Ice cruised around. I think it was something about us being in the dark looking out on the world, moving through the universe without being seen, our private wheels, our private space flight.

In between kissing on me Kicky was running her mouth with Bianca about some movie they had seen. It was almost as if I was background activity. Sometimes Ice got into the conversation but mostly it was just them talking to each other and Ice talking to me.

"We ought to get us a team," Ice said. "Remember that time we had the Great Five?"

"Yeah, we were going to play together and get great and then when we grew up we were going to join the NBA."

"That was a good idea," Ice said. "We just didn't know that you couldn't join the NBA."

"Ice, did you tell Bianca about that perfume?" Kicky asked.

"Yeah," Ice said. "Guy got the oils, you know, to make the perfume. He can match all the top brands. Anything you want he got for a pound an ounce."

"Me and Ice was thinking about getting some labels and making up some perfume for the black woman," Kicky said. "Then maybe we can get some guys to sell it outside the subways and stuff."

"How come you always got to have business with my man?" Bianca said.

"Don't even go there, girl," Kicky said. "Because nothing between me and Ice is on the program so you know it's not happening."

"Well, I just don't like to meet nothing that's my business coming round no corner," Bianca said.

"Hey, it's business," Ice said. "My nature don't come down for no stock exchange."

"That's all your nature's been coming down for lately," Bianca said.

"Yeah, right." Ice looked at Bianca and stepped on the gas. "I need to take you home, woman. You need to have stayed in your crib this morning if you woke up with an attitude that wrong."

We drove to Bianca's house on 137th Street and then we drove up to Eighth Avenue and 148th where Kicky lived. She lived one flight up and I walked her to her door. She kissed me again and told me how disappointed she was going to be if I didn't call her.

"Maybe we can double deal with Ice and Bianca if you and her make up," I said.

"She ain't mad at me because she know I don't mess with her man," Kicky said. "Maybe she got her month or something, I don't really know. You hear what I'm saying?"

I said I would call her and went on back downstairs to where Ice was waiting. I hopped into the front seat and we started driving around some more. It was like old times a little. He was telling me about his dreams and stuff. Mostly it was about how he was going to be in the NBA and get all the babes.

"The bucks you make in the NBA go past heavy," Ice said. "They get all the way to super light. You know why they super light?"

"Why?"

"Because you don't have to carry nothing around with you," he said. "All you carry is maybe four or five credit cards and pay everything with that. You walk into a store, you see a suit, and *Bam!* you order three of them — no, you order six of them in three different colors. You get your blue, your brown, and your gray. Then every time you fall out you fall out kicking. That's the way to live, my man."

"Drive around in a big 'chine like this one," I said.

"This ain't nothing," Ice said. "It belongs to this guy I know. I'm thinking about hooking up a Lexus. You know, get the basic model and then customize it. Put some way-out stuff in it, a CD changer, maybe a camcorder so I can record anything I pass. You ain't never seen no car with a built in camcorder."

"Hey, I hear you."

Ice drove me on home and I watched as he cruised away. The guy was exciting. I wondered what Mtisha would say if I cruised up in a Benz.

When I got home my moms was up doing the crossword puzzle. She said it was a stupid puzzle and she was going on to bed.

"Where were you?"

"Ice had to go out to Queens and I rode with him," I said.

"Ice has a car?" she asked, her arms folded in front of her.

"It was a friend's car," I said. "But he wheeled it like it was his sneakers."

"You boys should have been brothers," Moms said. "The way you get along with each other."

I gave her a peck on the cheek and headed for the crash zone. The chance for me to talk to Ice came and went and I didn't get up the nerve to talk to him. What was I going to say that he didn't know? Watch your back? Don't fall into no cracks? He didn't talk like he was dealing crack. Anyway, crack was the wrong road and anybody that lived in the hood knew where that was at, you don't have to teach fish to deal with water.

That was what my whole life was getting to be about, dealing with stuff going wrong that I knew about.

Mom came into my room with a Swiss cheese and tomato sandwich and asked if she could talk with me a while.

"So I'm going to have to work harder on the books," I said because I knew that was what was on her mind.

"Sometimes you can try something real hard," she said, "but you just can't get it all by yourself."

"You saying the teachers can't teach?" I asked.

"Don't talk with your mouth full," she said. "Just think about it. Maybe we can talk about it again?"

"Sure."

"You played good tonight," she said, standing in the doorway. "Everybody in the stands around me was talking about you. I was so proud."

"I didn't even know you were there," I said.

"I'm always there," she said. "And I'll always be there."

"Yo, I know that," I said. I sat up and pulled the spread around my shoulders. In the other bed Derek turned over and mumbled something in his sleep. When he was asleep his voice was deeper than when he was awake.

"Greg, I didn't mean to put your father down," she said. Her voice was soft. "And you certainly don't have to deal with Mr. Randall. I mentioned him to your father, today. I told him that Mr. Randall was an engineer and that he could help you with your math. He didn't seem to mind, but the decision is up to you. Okay?"

"Sure."

She blew me a kiss and closed the door.

I thought about the game. The feel of the ball in my hands was still there. I don't tell a lot of people but I like the little pebbles on the ball, the way they feel against my fingertips. Once I told Mtisha that the way the ball felt, the pebbles and the roundness where the seams are, almost felt like a woman to me. She said I must be hanging out with some hard-butt women. But later she came and said she was sorry. Never did figure out what she was sorry about.

Then there was me cruising with Ice. I took the ticket about the car being his friend's but I didn't go for the show. People don't just lend you a Benz because they think you're cool. Still, it was nice cruising around like that, just taking it like it comes. You sitting in the back of a car with your homeboy and maybe some babes and things just peace out for you.

Then I pushed my head back to the basketball game again and I couldn't wait to get to school the next day to see what everybody was saying. Getting to sleep was hard.

So we had to do this school project and we had to have a partner. Who I end up with is Margie. Her real name is Marjorie Flatley and I don't like her because she thinks she cute. She's got blonde hair and real big brown eyes. She plays piano, vibes, marimba, and anything else she can bang on. She's good, too. But she'll lay a diss on you like she's doing you a favor.

"So what do you want to do?" she asked me.

"I want to make a video," I said. "You know, how I live and stuff like that. What do you want to do?"

"I can deal with a documentary," she said. "You ever watch public television?"

"Yeah."

"Well, we'll get a video camera from the school's video department and shoot something," she said. She had a brush that had a mirror on the back of it and was checking herself out in the mirror and brushing her hair while she was talking.

"The story of Slam the Great," I said.

"That's okay. You can do the shooting," she said. "You do everything that's important to your life. Your neighborhood, your house, and where you shop and things like that. And then I'll edit it. The school has an editing machine. You have to shoot a lot of tape, like maybe ten hours. If you shoot a lot of tape I can edit it down to thirty minutes and put music to it."

"That's cool."

So that's how we decided what we were going to do. Me and Marge. I wasn't that down for working with Marge but it was something to do.

"Yo, Slam." It was Ducky.

"What's happening?"

"I may not be on the team much longer," he said. He shrugged his shoulders and got this crooked grin on his face.

"How come?"

"Glen said about five more guys came to the gym today and asked about being on the team," Ducky said. "After they saw you play the other night they all want to be on the team."

"So what's that got to do with you?" I asked. "You're already on the team."

"They'll probably play better than me," Ducky said. "Or if I don't get kicked off the team then I probably won't get to play anymore."

"You can play better than you're playing," I said. "You just got to work on it during practice, especially the way you handle the ball. You act like you're scared out there."

"Yeah."

He got his books out of his locker and went on down the hallway. It's funny the way some guys think they can just come out and play ball and don't work at it. And the way he walked away you could see he wasn't even going to try. He had it in his head that he wasn't going to make it.

The video department is on the fourth floor and I went there and told them I wanted to borrow a camera. They said I had to go down to the library and get a slip from Miss Fowell before I could get one. So I go down to the library and wait for like ten minutes for Miss Fowell to get back from somewhere and I asked her for a slip so I could get a video camera. Then she tells me I got to get a slip from Mr. Parrish, my English teacher, before she gives me a slip.

It was a little funny, really. I had to get a slip to get a slip to get a camera. So I tracked down Mr. Parrish and told him what I needed and he told me that he already gave Margie a slip.

So then I find Margie. No, first I found Vicky Garcia and told her I was looking for Margie and Vicky asked me if I was sweating Margie. Now what would I look like sweating Margie?

"No, I just need to get something from her," I said.

"She said you were always checking her out," Vicky said. "I don't know. Now you going round looking for her and everything."

Anyway, she told me that Margie was in the cafeteria because she had a early lunch.

On the way to the cafeteria five people stopped me to talk about the game and about nine or ten people waved to me. Yo, I wasn't just on the scene, I *was* the scene. Yeah. Even Miss Meade, the school nurse, stopped me and said she had heard about the game.

"I don't know how people can jump high enough to throw the ball down into the basket," she said.

That was cool. It wasn't true, but it was cool. She knew that guys slammed the pill, but she just said that to make me feel good. I felt good.

The day before the game everybody was looking at me like I was nothing and then after the game I was the man. It wasn't something that fell on me, either. It was me, burning on the court, doing the wild thing with the ball, slamming and jamming. Me. Just how bad I felt when they were looking at me like I wasn't nothing was just how good I felt when Miss Meade was talking to me.

When I left her I started thinking about some new moves. That was what I was thinking about and then I was thinking about facing Carver and going up against Ice. That was going to be a challenge. Ice could do everything but I couldn't let him get my game. I had to be ready when I went up against him.

It made me mad what Vicky said about me sweating Margie. I could see me sweating Vicky. Vicky was Puerto Rican and like super fine. You take away Margie's eyes and she wasn't anything special. Maybe she was sweating me. When I found out I was going to be working the project with her I thought it was just the way things were but maybe she worked it that way. Sometimes she was checking me out, too. It could have been like a Romeo and Juliet thing with her loving me the first time she saw me and thinking that we could be like big-time moviemakers and then go to Hollywood and be stars and whatnot. We could show up at the Oscars in a stretch limo and she'd be wearing this gown and I'd be in a tuxedo. That worked.

"Hey, Margie, you got a slip from Mr. Parrish for the video camera?" She was sitting with two other girls and they were looking at some magazines.

"Yeah, I gave it to the video camera department," she said. "I just missed you. They said all you got to do is to come pick up the camera."

Now how come all she had to do was to take the slip up to the video department and everything was everything and I had to go through all those changes? I went on up to the video department and got the camera.

"You know how to use it?"

"Yeah."

Which wasn't exactly true, but I didn't want to look dumb or nothing and I figured I could learn to use a camera. No big deal.

I also noticed how Margie didn't say anything about me checking her out. When a girl acts cool like that in front of her friends you know something is probably happening.

After school I showed Derek the camera and took some tape of him. He was clowning around and when we played the tape back I saw that it was too dark and I was jerking the camera around. But it was still fun. Derek wanted to tape me and I let him, then Mom came home and I taped her and Derek. We set up a scene with Moms and Derek playing like Derek was a customer and Mom was a used car salesman and they were bargaining over a car. It was funny because Derek was serious but Mom kept cracking up.

I couldn't wait to go out into the park and have Derek shoot me going to the hoop, but Moms needed me to go to the hospital with her to see Grandma.

We waited for a while until my pops came home so he could go with us but when he got home he had liquor on his breath and then he went and laid down. Moms didn't say anything but I know she was upset. Two years ago, when he lost his job, he was hitting the bottle heavy and once he was arrested on some jive charge.

We got to the hospital and me and Mom were on a up but when we saw Grandma it was a big-time crash. She looked awful.

"She had a bad night," the nurse said. "She had some fluid in her lungs and we had to drain that. That's what the tubes are for."

"Why's she sleeping?" I asked.

"When we put the tubes down her nasal passages she was gagging on them," the nurse said. "So we gave her a sedative. She can use the rest anyway."

Moms wanted to sit by the bed for a while and we did. Moms broke out into crying again, that soft kind of crying with her body doing more crying than her face. Most of the time I didn't think on dying and stuff, and I couldn't get next to it even with Grandma. It made me feel bad to see Moms break up, though.

The next day at practice Mr. Nipper said he wasn't going to put anybody else on the team unless there was an injury. I gave Ducky a wink and he winked back.

We ran some plays and I noticed that I was in a lot of them. When me and Ducky were in the same play I looked for him and got the pill to him sometime. He was still acting like he was afraid to get the ball. Maybe like he was more afraid of messing up than anything else.

"Hey, Slam, you want to go one-on-one?" Nick asked.

"Yeah, why not?"

I could deal with Nick's wanting to go one-on-one with me. He was the man before I got on the scene and he was looking to make a comeback, or maybe he was just looking to prove something to himself.

My sneakers were on the side where I had taken them off and I went over to put them back on. A couple of guys were shooting around and I knew they wanted to see what was going to go down between me and Nick. But then Jimmy came over and made believe he was picking up something in front of me.

"The coach told him to go one-on-one with you," he said.

Now what was that about?

When somebody jumps into your face on the court it's because they think he got your game in his pocket. Coach Nipper jumped into my face and I showed him he didn't have a game and there was no way he could get mine. Now he had Nick jumping up into my face. Maybe he thinks he's got something but all he sees is the outside of me, he hasn't even peeped inside, where the real game is.

"Five baskets wins," Nick said and bounces the ball to me so I can take it out. What I'm thinking is that the coach wants me to try to slam over Nick. Uh-uh. I didn't know what he had in mind, but he wasn't going to get it the way he was looking for it.

I moved on Nick and he came up and made contact with me. He wasn't laying on me, like the coach did, but he was bumping me light and keeping one leg back. That way he could move that leg quick if I try to get around him and he could use it for a quick step and jump if I tried to go over him. He was bumping and staying on top of me. I made a little fake and he didn't go for it completely, but he made a little half step. I tried to go around him once and he cut me off. But when he cut me off I was closer to the hoop.

I made another little move and I saw I could move him back toward the basket. He saw this, too, and pushed up stronger. I backed up, let him make his push, then blocked him out with my left elbow and put up a soft hook off the boards. I was one up.

He took the ball out and threw up a quick jumper that rimmed the hoop and came down to one side. He beat me to the bound and drove for a layup. I let him go. One to one.

He had to lose that way and he had to know he was going to lose that way. I backed him in again and he was pushing me with his hips and slapping after the ball. I spun on him and he backed off. All right, he didn't want me to go by him. So I backed him into the paint the same way I did the last time and this time I push him off with my right elbow and make a little left-hand hook. Two to one.

The rest of the team is standing on the side, watching us. I slammed on the coach and I slammed during the game so they were watching for my slam. Nick took the ball out and put it on the floor like he was going to go by me, then pulled up and took the jumper. *Swish*. All right, two to two and I got the program.

What he wanted to do was to get the step on me and throw it down. I never saw him dunk but that had to be the program. Nick knew and the coach knew he couldn't beat me one-on-one but if he dunked on me the coach was getting his comeback because he got Nick to jam on me. He was putting me into a picture he could deal with.

I took the ball out, drove into Nick, spun, got my left foot outside his left foot and muscled past him. He's a half-step behind but he's coming and I made the layup on the other side of the basket. Three to two.

Now Nick had pressure on him. He brought the ball in, took a dribble with his right hand, pulled up and brought his left hand toward the ball for the jumper. Soon as he touched the ball with both hands I get up in his face. He couldn't dribble again and he's too far away to shoot anything good.

He threw up a wild hook and I cut him off so he couldn't get the bound. I cut to it and I see he's not near me so I plant and fly. Slam!

"Go get him, Slam!" Glen calls out and Jimmy and Ducky are giving each other high fives.

The coach is still watching. It's four to two.

Now I know that Nick wanted to slam on me but when he took the ball out I didn't move. I just stood there on the side and let him go by me. He looked over at me and dug me smiling at him. He laid the ball up. Four to three.

I got my slam and I don't want to give him another shot so I backed him in again. He was on me hard, getting me with his knee and pushing me with his hips. I had all day, and I kept backing him in and leaning on him. Nick was strong and I was thinking about maybe throwing the ball off the backboard and going for the tap-in off the bound. But then he tried to swing around me and steal the ball and missed. I spun, cut him off with my elbow, and made the layup. All over. Lights out. I looked over at the coach and he was walking away.

"Nice game," I said to Nick.

He nodded but he didn't say nothing.

Jimmy walked me to the train station. Usually he hung out with the white kids and I wondered why he was walking with me.

"The coach said you have an attitude problem," he said.

"He told you that?"

"He wasn't talking to me." Jimmy leaned forward into the wind as he walked. "I heard him talking to some of the other guys."

"What you think?" I asked him. "You think I got an attitude problem?"

"Sometimes you act as if you have a chip on your shoulder," he said. "You know what I mean?"

"What did I do to you?"

"You didn't do anything to me," he said. "I'm just talking about in general. Most of the guys get along fairly well."

"What do you think I should do?" I asked.

"I don't think you should jam on your teammates," he said. "Just, you know, cool it a little. That's why I told you the coach told Nick to play you one-on-one."

"So I could act right?"

"Just act like you're part of the team," he said.

We didn't say anything else all the way to the subway. I just wanted to get away from Jimmy, just wanted to walk out of his life. What I felt like, too, was going upside his head. But I knew that was what he was talking about, me acting like I had a chip on my shoulder, doing what I could do instead of fitting in like they wanted me to fit.

The words had to be there somewhere, the words that would tell him how I felt without catching in my throat or showing how mad I was. What I had to do was to find them, maybe even practice them so I could lay them on him the next time we met.

"See you tomorrow," he said.

"Sure," I answered. "Sure."

CHAPTER SEVEN

Derek was getting ready to go to the hospital with Moms. She wanted him to put some coconut oil on his face because she thought his skin looked ashy. Derek didn't want coconut oil on his face because it stinks and he didn't care if his face does look ashy.

"You're going to the hospital to see your grandmother," Moms said. "You can at least look good."

"Yeah, man." I was putting the tape in the video machine. "Your face does look a little ashy."

"Slam, why don't you shut up?"

"How did school go today?" Moms asked me.

"Went okay," I said. "I was working hard."

She gave me a look and I gave her a smile but she wouldn't smile back. Derek grabbed a tissue off the counter before they left. By the time they reached the hospital that oil would be off his face. I kissed Moms good-bye.

It had to be hard to see your mother in the hospital and thinking she was going to die. It hurt even to think that Moms would be the one in the hospital and me and Derek would have to go see her.

There was some orange juice in the fridge and I poured myself a glass. Way back in the freezer, under some frozen chopped collard greens, and wrapped in aluminum foil, was something special I had saved for myself. I just hoped that Derek hadn't found it. I reached back and found it and opened it up. It had been a whole slice of sausage pizza but now it was only a half slice. Derek had found it and copped half. If he had ate the whole thing I would have had to knock him down and stomp on his chest.

I put the pizza on a plate and put it in the microwave. Somebody was knocking on the door and I yelled for them to come on in because I hadn't locked it. It was Mtisha.

"Yo, baby, what's happening?" I reached over to give her a kiss and she pushed me away.

"Where were you last night?"

"Last night?"

"What are you, an echo?"

"I was out with my boy, Ice," I said.

"And Bianca wasn't with him?"

"Yeah, she was with him," I said.

"And why do you think she lies the way she does?" Mtisha asked.

"I don't even know that she lies," I said, putting the pizza into the microwave.

"Then what she said about you and Kicky kissing in the backseat was the truth?"

"She said that?"

"I just told you she did."

"Oh."

"So you kissed Kicky?"

"Kicky?"

"So why did you kiss Kicky?" Mtisha's eyes were watered like she was fixing to cry. "Is she what you're looking for?"

"No, and I wasn't kissing her," I said.

"Bianca is downstairs," Mtisha said. "You want me to call her up here?"

"Hey, look, she was kissing me," I said.

Mtisha didn't say another word. She just turned around and walked out the door.

Man, I didn't know the girl was going to get all upset and everything like that. If I had known that I wouldn't have been kissing on no other woman. I

92

wanted to run after her so bad I didn't know what to do. I started out the door, went back and locked it, then started to bust down the stairs. By the time I got downstairs and to the front door she was halfway down the street. The only thing I could think of saying was how sorry I was, and I ran across the street, dodging in front of a cab, and finally catching up with her in front of the liquor store.

"Yo, Mtisha!"

"I don't want to hear it, Slam," she said.

"Look, I'm sorry," I said.

"If you got down on your knees I wouldn't care," she said, stopping and turning toward me.

Hey, that worked. I got down on one knee and took her hand in mine. "Baby, I'm sorry. I didn't think you were serious with me."

An old woman came over and looked down at me. "Don't give him no slack, honey," she said.

"Get out of here!" I yelled at her.

"I'm going," Mtisha said. "You don't have to yell at me."

"I'm talking to her, not you. You know nothing serious happened. I told her I didn't want to mess with her but she kept pushing herself on me," I said.

"No, that's not your problem," Mtisha said. "Your problem is that because I'm not doing for you what some of these girls will do for anybody you got to look over my shoulder. Well you can look over my shoulder all you want because I just don't care."

Yeah.

Okay, so Mtisha was out of my mind. If that's the way it had to be, then that's the way it had to be. I got down on my knees and told her I was sorry and she didn't give me a play. It was over. Life goes on. Tomorrow is a new day.

The pizza was burned up, hard as a rock. No, harder than that, hard as Mtisha's heart.

It was bad but it wasn't terrible. Mtisha was hurt but I didn't know she was going to be hurt like that. If I had known that I would have looked for her after the game. That's what's wrong with women. They want you to wait for them until they get ready and then they don't even tell you how they feel. Mtisha never looked in my eyes and just laid out how she felt, how much she loved me and everything.

The video camera was on my bed and I remembered what I was supposed to be doing. Mtisha was still on my mind but I figured I would work hard and forget about her until after supper and then I would call her on the phone and tell her how much

I loved her and how Kicky didn't mean nothing to me. Then what I should do is to call Bianca and ask her what her problem was. Who did she think she was? Channel 4 news or something? Ice better tell her to keep her attitude and her loose lips out of other people's business.

On the street I went down to the corner where the Arabs have their little store. I videotaped the outside of the store and then started working my way down the street. A woman in the beauty parlor waved to me and I shot up real close to the window. Then I shot some of the action in the car wash. Some of the brothers wiping down cars saw me and started putting on a show.

The stoops along 145th always looked more or less the same, cracked steps with people either standing on them or sitting on them because life got too depressing in their apartments.

One dude waved me off. He was probably wanted by the police or something. Four stoops in a row had kids on them and the fifth had some gang-bangers so I skipped them. They gave me a look anyway.

The guy in the West Indian restaurant called me in and I shot him standing over the stove. He was cooking cow feet stew and dirty rice. Two of his customers smiled at the camera and the last one didn't smile but she straightened up her coat and checked herself out in the mirror.

The way I figured it was that if Bianca told Mtisha about me and Kicky it was because she was mad at Kicky, not me. I knew Mtisha knew Bianca but I didn't think they were tight or anything like that.

What I hadn't done was to break down just how I felt for Mtisha. Usually I kidded around with her or maybe I got a quick kiss, but she was right, we never got into anything serious. I thought about telling her that I would wait until we got married. Then I thought that if she went to college that would be four years, four and a half if you thought about her finishing high school, too. That was a long time to wait for something you weren't sure you were going to get. No, I would just break it down the way I felt it. I could do that.

When I got down to Carl's Curio Shop he was talking to a girl who smelled like the toilet in a men's room. She was trying to sell him two shiny things. She had that glassy look in her eyes, the way that crack heads do.

"I don't even know what these are," Carl said.

"C'mon, baby," the girl said. "All I'm asking is a dollar."

"If I don't know what they are how am I going to sell them?" Carl asked, giving her back the shiny things.

"You need some affection today?" she asked him.

"No, I don't think so," Carl said. Then he reached under the counter and pulled out a dollar and gave it to her. She didn't say a word, just took the dollar and walked out.

"You know she used to have a tailor shop?" Carl asked.

"Her?" I couldn't believe that anybody that looked that bad and smelled that bad could have had a shop of any kind.

"Then she found the pipe," Carl said. "Or maybe the pipe found her. Anyway, they still together."

"Her and the pipe?"

"Yeah."

I shot around Carl's shop and then I went down and shot the two pit bulls outside the bicycle shop. There was a red light flashing in the camera. The battery was probably low. The battery had been charging all day but Derek was probably messing with the camera even though Moms told him to keep his hands off it.

I went upstairs and called Mtisha. Her mother answered the phone and called me a lowlife.

"I thought you had more to you than that, Slam," she said.

"Can I speak to Mtisha?"

"No."

"Will you tell her I'm sorry?"

"No."

"Okay, just tell her that I didn't date Kicky," I said. "She was with Ice."

"Was Ice the one in the backseat kissing her?" Mrs. Clark asked.

I wish the heck he had been.

CHAPTER EIGHT

The whole weekend I spent doing two things, playing ball at the 135th Street YMCA and shooting some videotape around 125th Street. The games went good because there's always some smoking brothers playing at the Y. At the Y if you can't get down you got to watch. I played with some guys who had played college ball and they were good. One guy even played in Italy for a while. His name was Kenny Stith and he said his uncle used to play with the Knicks. I don't know about that but I knew the dude could play.

What I didn't understand was how he could be so good and not be in the NBA, so I asked him when we were taking a break.

"Being good in the NBA don't mean nothing," he said. "Everybody's good in the NBA."

"Then how you get a play?"

"You got to be better than good, and you got to be hungry all the time," Stith said. "If you thinking about anything else than getting the ball and winning the game you gone."

"How you like my game?" I asked him.

"You okay," he said. "You in college?"

"No, man, I'm just in high school," I said.

"You got a sweet game for high school," he said.

That made me feel good. And when we got back on the court I really busted it. The jumper was on. I went up on this one dude who had blocked a few shots and it was like I didn't have any weight at all. I just floated to the top of my leap, stopped and let the ball go. The ball went through the rim, stopped for a second as it got caught up in the net, and fell through gently as I headed downcourt.

After the game I saw Kenny talking to a girl and a kid. When he was leaving he was carrying the kid so I figured it must have been his. When I get to the NBA I'm just going to keep concentrating on ball. No wife. No kids. Maybe it was cool that Mtisha put me down. A sign or something. She was definitely wrong, though. I didn't come on to Kicky she came on to me. If I hadn't kissed her back she'd be running it down that I was freak or something. Sometimes any way you go you wrong.

Monday morning and it's New Year's Day. This was going to be a fresh start. I called Mtisha and she answered the phone. All the cool stuff I was going to say just flew out my head and I heard myself begging for just one more chance. She said she would think about it.

Okay. So I get to the NBA and I'll have a wife, maybe a kid. Probably a boy.

Tuesday after New Year's and I'm busting into school thinking about the game we were going to have that afternoon against St. Peter's. I kind of skate through the announcements and homeroom and then I'm dozing in history. In my mind I fast-forward to the end of the day even though I know I got math. What I don't know is we got a math test.

"It's a four-part test," Mr. Greene said. "You *will* get partial credit so make sure all of your work is on the paper you hand in. This will make up twenty-five percent of your final grade, so be careful. You can leave whenever you're finished."

My stomach tightened up real bad. When I looked at the problems it got even worse.

1. $-2X - 5 + 12X - 3 - 4 = 8$ solve for X
2. $X/2 - X/3 + 7 = 5X/6 - 5$ solve for X
3. Pete, Jane, and Bill all worked on the same job, but for different rates of pay. Pete

gets twice the amount that Jane gets, and three times the amount that Bill gets. How much does each worker get if they get a total of $1,254 dollars?

4.   Mary is two times $(4 + 15/X)$ years old. Her identical twin Chris is almost fifteen. Solve for X.

I couldn't believe Mr. Greene was serious. I just kept looking at the numbers and they didn't mean nothing to me. We had gone over the problems in class but the way it looked in front of me didn't make sense. I looked up at Mr. Greene and he was looking dead at me.

The last problem looked the easiest so I tried to do that one first. Mary is two times (4 + fifteen over X). She had to be more than eight because she was two times four plus something else. Then her twin brother was almost fifteen. That meant that he was fourteen and since that was her twin brother it made her almost fifteen, too. That meant she was fourteen.

There wasn't any fourteen in the problem but there was a two times four which was eight. So the rest of it had to be six. But I didn't know where the X come in. Mr. Greene went to the door and I took a look over to where Ducky sat. He wasn't up to number four yet.

Then I went to number three. For a long time it didn't make any sense at all. I remembered Mr. Greene putting a problem like it on the board. Then I figured that X is what I was looking for. Pete got three times more than Bill so I put down 3X. Then he got two times more than Jane so I put down 2X. Then I put down just plain X for the last amount. That added up to 6X and I made that equal to $1,254. Then I divided $1,254 by 6 and got $209. Then I figured that Pete got the most so I gave him three times $209 which was $627. Jane got the next so she got two times $209 which was $418. Then Bill got the least which was only one X and that was $209. I added up the $627, the $418, and the $209 and it came up to $1,254, which was right.

Margie got up and left. She handed her paper to Mr. Greene and she was smiling. Then two more kids got up and left. The questions wasn't *that* easy.

Number one was okay since it was negatives and positives and those aren't too bad. Number two had fractions in it and they were hard unless they were all the same. You can make them all the same if you multiply by the right number. I remembered something like that, or maybe it was divide them all by the same number.

At the beginning of the year Mr. Greene went through a whole day talking about how we could use math. He was showing us how everything we did had some math in it. He said that if you went to the moon you would have to figure out things using math and if you went to the corner store you would have to do math, too. If I had to go to the corner store and do fractions I wouldn't even bother going, I'd just look for a store that didn't have fractions.

Sixty-five was the passing grade and I needed some credit on each of the problems if I was going to pass. I divided 65 by 4 and got 16.25. Each part had 25 points to add up to a hundred and I needed 16.25 out of each part. If I only got partial credit for three then I would have to divide 65 by 3. I did that and it come out to 21.66. That means I had to get them almost right. So if I got three almost right I would pass. And then if I got three almost right and did okay on the other one I would be fine.

I looked my work over. Number one, three, and four looked almost right to me. But now I knew I had to do something to get partial credit on number two, just to make sure.

I decided to change the fractions to sixes. That

made the problem X over six minus another X over six, which didn't look right because first I had two different numbers and now I had the same number.

Carol O'Connor, who used to go to Catholic school, got up and turned her paper in and then just about everybody else was standing up. I didn't want to be the last one to go.

Glen stood to go and I looked over and saw his answer for the second problem. It was 18. I looked back at my paper and tried to figure out how he got 18. Then I saw it. You multiplied the tops of the equations and you got to minus X over six. Then when you brought that over to the other side it was a plus X over six which made that number six X over six. Then you brought the minus five over to the other side, changed the signs, and made that a plus twelve. So then you got to six X over six equals twelve. Glen was wrong.

Six X over six equals X. X equals twelve was the answer. I put that down and then I got up and turned my paper in.

In the hallway some of the kids were talking about how easy a test it was. It wasn't that easy, I knew that. But I figured I did okay on it. When I was taking it I was looking for the answer and I didn't know if I got it right or not, but that's how those tests go. You look around for something that looks like the answer and then you go with that. Sometimes you're right. When you get partial credit that's good. At least it shows you know something.

In the locker room the test was still on my mind. It was only part over. The part of taking it was over but then the next day, or whenever Mr. Greene marked the papers, was the rest of it.

"Hey, there's a guy with a dog in the stands," Charley Movalli said when we got into the gym.

The guy was sitting there with a Seeing Eye dog and a white cane. He was kind of a good-looking guy, distinguished.

"That's Trip's father," Ducky said.

"Get out of here!"

"No, that's his father," Ducky said. "He lost his sight in the army. There was an explosion in the barracks, Lebanon or some place like that, and he was blinded."

That was cold. Losing your sight was nasty.

We shot around for a while and then the guys from St. Peter's showed up. They had one dude who was so fat I had to laugh. Guy looked like he should have been a football player, or better than that he could have just stood on the curb and been a fireplug. They didn't look like anything to worry about.

The coach called us over and told us to start our warm-ups.

I felt good. We formed two lines and ran layups for a while and then Nick started shooting from the outside and we all switched to that. St. Peter's was running the same lines that we had ran but they had a nice little twist to theirs. One guy would throw the ball off the board and the guy in the other line would tap it in. I liked that.

They didn't make all their taps but they made a lot and I thought they might not be scrubs after all. They had some height but their big men were skinny.

"Yo, here comes our band!" Jimmy said.

I looked over and saw a group of kids coming through the door with instruments. They started setting up and I saw that they had six violins, two clarinets, a marching snare, Marjorie on a portable keyboard, and two flutes. The ref blew the whistle and gave us the signal for the game to start.

"Okay, Trip and Nick at guard, and I want you to keep the defensive pressure on these guys. They want to play a half-court game, they don't want to play the whole court . . ."

He went on but I didn't want to hear. I still wasn't starting. What was wrong with the man?

I looked up in the stands and there wasn't anybody I knew there. I mean, there were most of the kids I knew from Latimer but nobody from the hood.

The team went out on the floor and Ducky found me and sat next to me.

"Maybe he's mad because you beat him that time," he said.

"Or maybe he's just stupid," I said.

St. Peter's got the tap and right away their forwards came out to the top of the key. The guards passed the ball into the forwards and then moved into the forward spots and the two guys who had lined up at forward were now playing guard. Cute.

Nick and Trip didn't know whether to go out to play the first guys they had or stay with the new guards. The coach stood up and looked at his clipboard as St. Peter's rotated again, but this time their center picked Trip deep and they got an easy bucket.

This was going to be one of those tricky games.

St. Peter's started with a two-one-two zone defense. That's when I saw that the fat dude on their team was playing center. He wasn't tall, and he wasn't quick, just fat. And strong. He was pushing Jimmy all over the place. Trip tried to get inside but the inside zone picked him up and he passed to

Jimmy who was standing alone at the top of the key. Jimmy threw up a three and caught nothing but net and everybody on our side of the gym went off.

"Good shot, Jimmy!" the coach yelled as Jimmy started backing down the court on D.

Behind us our band started playing. They were playing the theme from *The Lone Ranger* and they were kicking it pretty good.

The St. Peter's team was called the Marauders. Two guys brought the ball down and then the two guys who had hustled down into the forward slots came out and took the ball. They were going to play that game all day about who were the guards and who weren't. I could see Trip glance toward the coach.

We were still in a man-to-man and they worked the ball around until their big man, I mean their fat man, picked off one of our guys and they had another easy two.

We brought the ball down and as soon as Jimmy touched the ball he turned and threw up his second three-pointer.

"Way to go Jimmy!"

We were up six to four, but our center was shooting threes. You don't win no game with your center shooting threes.

CHAPTER NINE

The next few times up and down the court and St. Peter's was moving ahead slow without playing any real ball. They were bringing their forwards out, sending their guards into the low post, and using their center for some picks that looked illegal to me but the referee didn't call them. A couple of times I saw Jimmy and Frank looking over at me. They were wondering the same thing I was, when was I going in.

At halftime St. Peter's was ahead 32–22.

I looked in the stands and saw Trip's father. He had his chin on the handle of his cane. There was a girl sitting next to him. I figured she was telling him about the game. I wondered if she was telling him how bad we was playing.

In the locker room the coach was talking about

how we had to overload one side of their zone and block off the defense when we swung it to that side.

"Hey, Coach, how come Slam isn't in the game?" Glen asked the question.

"Because we need a whole team of players, not just one guy," the coach said. "Everybody will play if and when the opportunity comes."

I didn't go for it, and I could tell the rest of the team didn't either. Nobody said much, we just hung in the locker room until it was time to go out for the second half. We started warming up and Goldy came up to me.

"You want to play the second half?" he asked.

"What's up with this 'you want to play' bit?" I asked.

"The coach thinks you're a hot dog," Goldy said. "He thinks you're more interested in showing off your stuff than playing with the team."

"I think he's mad because I slammed on him," I said.

"Could be," Goldy said. "But that's real life. What did you expect?"

"What do you mean?"

"He thought he could take you and you showed him up," Goldy said. "You expect him to like it?"

111

"That ain't got nothing to do with playing today," I said. The coach was playing with *my* mind because *his* game was raggedy. I didn't even know how to deal with that.

I turned and threw up a jumper that didn't even reach the rim. Then I chased the ball down, and threw up another jumper. Blew that sucker, too. Goldy came over to me.

"Get into the game," he said. "Whenever he lets you play, get into the game and show what you got. They can argue with what you say, but nobody can argue with what you accomplish. You see what I mean?"

I didn't say nothing and Goldy walked away. I blew another jumper and went and sat down next to Ducky. I put a towel over my head.

"What's the matter?" Ducky asked.

"What you think is the matter?"

"You're not playing?"

"You must be Einstein or somebody," I said.

The second half started with me sitting on the bench. The coach looked over at me and I looked the other way. If he was expecting me to show humble he was wrong big time.

St. Peter's was trying the same things they did in the first half and we were in the same zone, but still standing around trying to figure out who they were playing where. We were down 42–30 with eight minutes to play when the coach signals me to go in.

"Get 'em, Slam," Ducky called out.

"Move that guy out of the center," I told Jimmy.

"You're not the coach," he said.

"Move him or I'll break your jaw after the game!" I said. Jimmy really pissed me off. He knew the game was getting away and that was why the coach put me in, and he was still going to come down lame.

The first time I got my hands on the ball I knew I was going to make them know I was there. I went right toward their big man, and when he stepped out I faked left and drove around his right side. Their forward came over quick but he was a step late so he could have kept his butt home. I went up, did a 180 and slammed backwards. The crowd went wild and they called a time-out.

Goldy and the coach went over to the scorer's tables to check on the time-outs. That's when Nick got into my face.

"Hey, you don't have any right to jump on Jimmy," he said.

"I'm taking the right," I came back.

"Well, if you throw down with him you got to throw down with me, too," he said.

"Then it's two against two," Ducky said. "I'm fighting with Slam."

"So when we doing it?" I asked.

"Hey, let's cool it," Jose stepped in between us as Goldy and the coach came back.

I didn't want to hear nothing from nobody. When the game started again I went into my bag and pulled out my whole act. They dropped their fat boy deep into the paint to clog up the middle but I just went over him. When they sent the fat boy and a forward into the paint I pulled up and dropped the pill from the top of the key. Nick didn't want me to have the whole show so he started doing his thing, too. That was okay with me, he could have anything left over after I did mine.

With thirty seconds to go it was 51–51 and they had the ball. Everybody knew they were going to hold it for one shot. Their point guard was quick but he was skinny. I went out after him and put my hand on his hip. I could stop him from going to his right just by pushing him a little. The referee was watching close and I knew he was looking for me to push too much and he would call a foul. It got down to fifteen seconds and I reached my hand up like I was going to push the guard again but instead I swiped after the ball. He braced himself for an instant and I got a fingertip on the ball.

It only went three feet away from him but it was like five feet from me. I started to dive but then something went past me like a shot.

Nick scooped the ball right into his dribble and was gone. Their guard went after him. The dude was quick. He got to Nick just as he reached our basket and fouled him as the buzzer sounded.

Our bench was on its feet and so was the St. Peter's bench. There wasn't any need to line up. All Nick had to do was make one of the foul shots and we had the game.

For some reason I thought Nick might blow the shot. He wiped his neck off with a towel and then went to the line. The ref gave him the ball and he looked like he was nonchalanting the shot. The ball went up, hit the front rim, rolled around twice, and then fell through. Case closed.

Nick made the second shot, too, but by then we were shaking hands with St. Peter's. They were pissed off because they thought they had the game before I got it. Good.

After the game two things happened. The first was that Goldy called me over.

"Nice game," he said. "You won it for us."

"Maybe I'll even start one day," I answered.

"I spoke to Mr. Greene, your math teacher," he said. "He said he had a lot of trouble giving you a thirty-four on your math test. It was all partial credit. If you don't get your grades together you won't even be on the team."

"I know the coach won't mind that," I said.

"Yeah, well when you see me tomorrow you tell me how that's going to help you. Okay?"

That got me down. Really down. Then the next thing happened. I got to the corner and Jimmy was there barking at Ducky. Nick was there, too. He was getting between them like he was stopping Jimmy from punching out Ducky.

Now Jimmy is an inch taller than me. I'm six four so that puts him at six five, maybe six five and a half. Ducky is like a foot shorter.

I didn't say anything. I just went up and put my hand in Jimmy's face and pushed him away.

"Yo, cool out!" Nick puts his books down and Ducky tackles him around the waist.

Then Jimmy, the center of our team, punks out and runs. I turned back to Nick and Ducky and they're still wrestling around. I grabbed Nick from the back and spun him off of Ducky into a parked car. He gets to his feet and puts his hands up and I just stand there. Because I know if he throws on me I'm going to light him up.

"Here comes Mr. Tate!" somebody behind me called out.

I looked down the street and Mr. Tate was walking with another teacher. He hadn't seen the fight yet. I looked over at Nick and he was picking up his books. Me and Ducky went on down the street.

"We got to get this straightened up," Ducky said. "It won't help the team. I'll call Nick tonight."

"Yeah. Right."

On the way home I should have been up but I was really down. It was getting colder. I pulled my coat around my neck and tried to think about the game, but all I could think about was the fight.

Sometimes, when I thought about what I was going to do with my life I would think about being a doctor or a lawyer and having a dynamite crib and either Mtisha or some movie star by my side. In my dreams it wouldn't all be front, either, it would be real world and real time.

But all that was big-time dreaming. Then something would happen like the fight or the math test and there would be a serious wakeup call. Then the only thing I could dream about is being on the same corner as the other brothers, looking for something to hook into. Maybe a laugh or a high. Same difference.

I knew in my heart I hadn't done anything on the math test. I had told myself that maybe I had got enough partial credit but I knew if I did it was just luck. Now Mr. Tate could sit there behind his desk and talk about me like I wasn't nothing and he would have it down in black and white so he could show it to me. Sometimes school was just this humongous diss you had to wear around your neck so everybody could check it out.

When I got to the hood the lights were on in the park. It was too cold to hope for a game but I got my ball and went out anyway. The park was just about empty and I moved around the key putting up jumpers that rattled against the old metal backboard. Some kids were watching me and one of them asked me if I could jam.

"Yeah, I can jam," I said.

"Let's see you." The little brother was dark and long-headed.

I went out to the top of the key, moved across the line slowly, then took a big step and went up. My jacket was too tight and I lost the ball on the way up.

"He can't even jam," one of the other little boys

said. They turned and started toward the other basket.

I don't know why it was important to jam. But I took off my jacket and my shirt. I bounced the ball hard a couple of times and when the kids turned around I started my move to the basket. I went up and slammed with one hand. I got the ball back, went out to the foul line, and came right back and did a two-handed slam. Then I slammed with my left hand and then I slammed with my right hand and then I threw the ball against the boards and went up and slammed the bound.

"He can really jam!" one of the kids said.

"Man, he something else!"

They went onto the next court and started their own hoop dreams. I watched them through the fence until I had calmed down enough to feel the cold again. The brief high had worn off.

The phone was ringing when I got home. Derek ran to it before I could get up and tell him not to answer it. If Mr. Tate had found out already and was calling, I didn't want to deal with the stuff until tomorrow.

"Hey, it's Mtisha."

The phone was in the living room and I got on the couch and picked up the receiver. Like Derek said, it was Mtisha.

"How you doing?" she asked.

"Not too good," I said. "Messing up."

"In school?"

"Yeah, I got a thirty-four on the math test," I said.

"How you feel about that?"

"Bad. No other way to feel," I said. "Hey, can I say something to you?"

"I really don't want to get into a heavy conversation," Mtisha said. "My moms wants to go visit your grandmother and I just wanted to know if you knew the visiting hours."

"Not exactly," I said. "We just went after school. It's probably until seven or eight. Your mother knows my grandmother?"

"Yeah, they both go to Pilgrim Baptist," Mtisha said. "What did you want to say?"

"Say?"

"You said you wanted to say something to me."

"Oh, yeah, like I'm sorry about Kicky," I said. "That shouldn't have happened. I didn't know — I knew what to do but I just didn't do it."

"Now you feeling sorry for yourself so you want to plea bargain your way back to me?"

"No . . . I mean, yeah," I said. "Look, I tell you the truth, girl, I ain't doing nothing right in my life these days."

"You want to go with us to the hospital and then we can talk about it?" she asked.

"I'm feeling so bad maybe I should just wait until tomorrow," I said. "I'll probably just say something stupid and get you mad again."

"Yeah, well I feel kind of bad about our argument, too," Mtisha said. "You know it wasn't even about Kicky. I mean I might kick her butt and all but it's not really about her."

"So what was it about?"

"Just trying to figure out how we all fit together," she said. "You know, me, you, Ice, Bianca, all of us. Cutting people out of your life is easy, keeping them in is hard."

"You thinking about cutting me loose?"

Mtisha said no, that she wasn't thinking about cutting me loose, but there was a moment of hesitation before she said it. I didn't want to push it because I wasn't ready, really ready, for no more hurt.

"When can I see you?" I asked.

"I don't know," she answered. "How sweet were those kisses Kicky forced on you?"

"Told you there wasn't anything going on between us," I said.

"I didn't say there was," Mtisha said. "I just need to know how hard I got to work my show. You hear what I'm saying?"

"Look, I love you."

There was the hesitation again.

"You getting heavy on me?"

"Something like that."

"Maybe I'll see you tomorrow," she said.

Yeah.

CHAPTER TEN

Derek was sitting on my bed when I woke up in the morning.

"Get off the bed."

"Let's go up on the roof and shoot some videotape," he said.

"What time is it?"

"Six-thirty," he said. "I saw that in the movies. They shot the start of the movie from the roof. Then they went down in the street and shot the same thing. It was cool."

"You saw that in the movies?"

"Uh-huh."

I got dressed and we went up to the roof. It really stunk. I don't think anybody ever cleaned it. There was a cardboard box and I knew somebody was sleeping in it. We went to the edge and looked down. The hood looked nice from the roof. I could see people starting off to work, a few guys who had been out all night collecting cans were coming back, and some people had already found them a spot on the stoop. I shot it all.

"Look over there."

Derek was pointing at an open window. There was this real fat guy sleeping in it and he didn't have a thing on but sneakers and a doo-rag. He could have been a real whale. Every time he breathed his stomach went up and down.

"Why he sleeping in his sneakers?" Derek asked.

"Maybe he's a sleepwalker," I said.

"If he walk out the house in nothing but his sneakers and a doo-rag he's gonna scare everybody to death," Derek said. "I bet his hair don't look like nothing either."

"Some guys just like wearing the doo-rag," I said. "They keep it on all the time and don't even care what their hair looks like."

Derek kept running his mouth about the whale dude and I shot some more tape. A beer truck came up and I saw it was for the bodega on the corner. The guy unloaded some cases of beer and took them on into the store. If he didn't look up I would see him and maybe even get him down on tape and I'd have him forever and he wouldn't even know it.

Things down in the street were small so it did look like a real movie. Nice.

Got back downstairs and Moms was making eggs.

"I don't want any eggs," Derek said.

"Did I ask you if you wanted eggs?" Moms said.

"Who you making them for?"

"You."

"You're going to make my cholesterol go up," Derek said.

"That's the way life goes," Moms said. "Sometimes you just can't win."

"When I grow up I'll never eat eggs."

Pops came out in his bathrobe and grunted.

"Yo, Daddy, what you think about me being a moviemaker?" Derek asked.

Pops grunted.

"Jimmy, the boy asked you a civil question," Moms said. "You can at least give him a civil answer."

"Be anything you want to be," Pops said to Derek. Moms had put a cup of coffee down in front of him and he put too much sugar in it the way he always did, then he just stirred right on top like he always did.

"Dad, how come you let all the sugar stay on the bottom?" Derek asked. "You don't never stir the bottom."

"Who drinking this coffee?" Pops asked.

"Your father woke up on the wrong side of the bed this morning," Moms said.

"I just ain't interested in nobody coming to my house and being no big brother to any of my kids," Pops said. "If I ain't his father he can't be no brother to one of my kids."

"All he wants to do is to help Greg in math," Moms said. "You don't know the kind of math they're teaching these days."

"If he wants to come to my house and see about what's going on here he should have got my name and called me. I don't know what he's talking to you for. I'm the man in my house."

"It's not about being a man, Jimmy." Moms voice started rising.

I didn't want to hear no more about that guy who was supposed to be tutoring me. I went on in the room and started dressing for school. In a way I could see where Moms was coming from, that it wasn't about manhood or nothing like that. But in the hood that manhood thing was like that card game they play on the corners downtown. Dude got three cards, two black and one red, and you got to find the red one. He mixes them up and you know you're not going to find the right one. People telling you that this ain't about manhood and that ain't about manhood and you end up trying to figure out what you got that is about manhood.

When I got ready to go Moms asked me how I felt about the tutor.

"You heard what Pops said."

"And what do *you* say?"

"I got to get to school."

In school there were announcements about everything in the world. Then the same girl that lost her wallet three times already lost it again and come on with the same crying voice saying how terrible she felt 'cause it was missing.

The morning took forever but nobody ran anything down about the fight. I found Ducky and asked him if he called Nick.

"Yeah, he said he didn't like you pushing people around," Ducky said. "I asked him what his problem was and he started talking about how he didn't have a problem."

"Then what did you say?"

"I told him he wanted to be the star of the team and he was pissed because you were. He didn't say anything about you after that. He just said he was going to forget about the fight."

"Uh-huh. If he's got a problem with me he'd better just get over it."

"I didn't think he wanted to fight yesterday," Ducky said.

"Yeah, but what were you doing with your little narrow butt jumping into a fight?" I asked. "'Cause you can't fight."

"Beats me," Ducky said. "I was wondering about that myself. Then I thought that maybe you and me are alike a little."

"How you figure?"

"We're just so good on the court everybody keeps watching us," Ducky said, grinning. "I'm thinking about slamming if I get in the next game."

"You better think about protecting the ball on the dribble," I said. "You don't work on that at all, do you?"

"You don't work at it."

"Yeah, I do. Whenever I play, even in the playground, I'm checking out how to protect the ball and do all the other stuff I do. You got to work on your game, man."

In English I told Margie I had brought some tape I had shot and she found me at lunch and dragged me to the video room. Karen Ballard was there, too, and she come over. I popped the video into the VCR and pushed play.

"We'll have to edit the tape first," Margie was saying. "Then we'll add music."

The tape started with me going down the street around from the fried chicken joint and then along the stoops. My man Web was in the shot in the car wash. I swear I didn't even see the sucker when I was shooting it because I was shooting a guy who was washing down a Jeep. Web was clowning on the side and flashing gang signals.

"This is where you live?" Margie asked.

"No, down the street," I said.

"This is really the ghetto!" she said.

"What are you trying to show?" Karen asked. "Is this supposed to be like a slice of life?"

"What's that supposed to mean?"

"I think it's good," Margie was saying. "You can put some jazz or something to it. Are these all abandoned houses?"

"People live in there," I said.

"This is going to be so good." Margie was shaking her head. "We might even get this on regular television."

She was saying it was good but I could see she was looking at it like she was front-rowing a freak

129

show or something. I just kept watching the screen and listening to her stupid comments. When the part came on with me and Derek up on the roof and she saw the whale guy she stopped the tape and played it back a couple of times. And every time she played it over she goofed on it like it was so way out. I turned the television off and took the tape out.

"What are you doing?" she asked.

"I'm not sure if this is the stuff I want in the video," I said. Then I just walked out with her talking at me in the background.

After school I met Mtisha and we walked down to the Schomburg on 135th Street. I started running my mouth to her and I couldn't shut up. I told her about the math test, the fight, about my pops getting uptight about the tutor, and last about Margie.

"Man, you're letting everything mess with you," she said. "You need to have your emotional immune system checked out."

"I need to have something checked out."

"So, have you seen Ice?" Mtisha waved at a girl she knew. When she waved she was smiling and she looked good as she wanted to.

"No, I was thinking about calling him tonight," I lied.

We got to the Schomburg library and went downstairs to the reference room. I showed Mtisha the math test that Mr. Greene had given me. The 34 was in red, underlined, and circled. Maybe he thought I was going to miss it or read it like it was 43 or something.

"What did he give you partial credit for? Neatness?" Mtisha asked.

"I probably got some parts right," I said.

"You're lucky I'm not your teacher. Look, if you don't want to deal with the tutor from the school why don't you get some guys from the basketball team to help you? Any homeboys on the team?"

"I can't ask some strange dudes for help like I'm some lame," I said. "Anyway I just had a fight with the one black dude on the team."

"Why don't you come to my house every day and we can do the homework together?"

"You know how to do these problems?"

"I can deal with them," she said. "We can start tomorrow. Today I have to find some books on black soldiers in the Civil War. You going to help me?"

"Sure."

We went to the computer and Mtisha started searching for black soldiers. She was racing through the files so fast I could hardly keep up with what she was doing. She made out a slip for the books she wanted and then started reading a magazine article that the librarian gave her about the Civil War.

She made me feel good in a way, all serious and everything. But in another way she made me nervous because I kept wondering if one day she was going to look at me and think she had to cut me loose because I wasn't smart enough, or I didn't make enough money. If we did hook up and we had a kid she could help him with his math, but if she didn't have time or something then what would happen? I looked over the math test again. I didn't even want her to know how much I didn't know. That was wrong, but that was where I was.

I knew if I went home after we left the library I wouldn't call Ice, so after I dropped Mtisha off I cut toward where he hung. All the time I'm walking down to his crib I'm thinking how I know I should talk to him because he's my ace and then I don't want to talk to him for the same reason.

V. J. Records is right next to Ice's crib and he was standing out in front of it. Soon as I saw him I got uptight. My stomach felt funny, like I was going to throw up.

Ice was wearing a tan Kangol to one side of his head. There were snowflakes falling and a few landed on his hat and turned to water. We talked about the Knicks and how we were going to cop some tickets for the Garden when the Chicago Bulls came in.

It was just light stuff, like the snow, falling around our heads and not sticking and I knew I wasn't going anywhere with the conversation.

Two street dudes came by, and one of them came over to us while the other one stood near the curb.

"What you want?" There was an angry edge to Ice's voice.

"Just looking to get right," the guy said. He looked old, a ghost with eyes that shone from the shadows of his face.

"I don't know what you talking about," Ice said. He looked away from the guy, down the avenue.

"I need a dime, man." The ghost's eyes were wide, desperate.

Ice shook his head and the thin man at his side rubbed his hands together, nodded, and walked away.

The two guys hooked up at the curb and put their heads together, looked back at Ice, then moved on.

"If you look like you got something going on, everybody think you got a pocket full of reefer or something," Ice said. "Look, you want to run over to Sylvia's for some pie?"

"No, I got to get back uptown," I said. "What you doing tomorrow? Maybe we can find some hangout time."

"Bet," he said. "I'll call you."

I started walking uptown as Ice headed toward V. J.'s. The two guys I had seen before were on the corner. I turned away from them as I passed.

Ice was dressed down and he had his cellular phone and his beeper working. I wasn't sure if he was using, but I knew the brother was dealing.

I wondered if Carl was right, that we were all getting so uptight about dope that anytime a brother dressed good we automatically put him in the life. It could have been like when somebody lost a lot of weight. They could have been on a dynamite diet but the first thing that came to mind was they got AIDS.

All the way home I was having a conversation with myself, saying how I had to give Ice his propers and not be laying nothing on him that wasn't for real. That's what happened to brothers in the hood. People check us out and ran down who we was without even seriously checking us out. I wouldn't play that game on Ice.

For a while I thought something was following me, but when I turned around there wasn't nothing there. Still I couldn't shake the feeling and kept looking over my shoulder. Maybe it was the way that people turned into shadows as it got darker or maybe it was just the wind at my back, blowing through the hood like it owned it, making things colder, reminding me that it owned the streets.

CHAPTER ELEVEN

When Nick Young came over to me in the lunch room I didn't know what he was going to do. I was pretty sure I could beat him in a fight, but I didn't really want to fight him. He had a sandwich that he had picked up outside and he sat down and took it out.

"So, you want to fight, or what?" he asked.

"Up to you," I said. "Don't make no difference to me."

"You think everybody's scared of you because you're black?" he asked.

Karen started to sit with us and Nick waved her off.

"You can be scared of me or not scared of me," I said. "But you're not going to mess with me. And if we need to go to war for you to understand that then we have to go to war."

"You started up with Jimmy when it wasn't anything really going on," Nick said. "He was trying to school you on how to get along."

"Yo, you better check your dance card again," I said. "Because I don't need to dance with you or Jimmy. And as far as I'm concerned the whole thing is that you don't dig my game. That's not my problem."

"I dig your game but I don't dig your attitude," Nick said. "You're one of these people who thinks the world owes you a living. Nobody owes you so much you can go around pushing people around. "

"But Jimmy can push Ducky around, huh?"

"Wasn't anything happening there," Nick said. "That was light. You made it heavy."

"It was light because Ducky is weak," I said. "When I stepped up Jimmy ran like a punk. Ain't that right?"

Nick looked away. "Maybe," he said, "but nobody owes you a living. Your game's not that tough."

We had two games in two days. Friday we were going to play Country Day, then on Saturday afternoon we were going to play Trinity. Mr. Greene gave us a lot of homework over the weekend and Glen told him that he wouldn't have a chance to get it done because of the ball game.

"Then you'll probably have a lot more time when you take math over the summer," Mr. Greene said.

That was cold.

Country Day had some nice uniforms but they didn't have anybody on their team who was all that. All they did was to pass the ball around the outside and look for an open jumper. Nick was scrambling all over the place on defense and Jimmy was steady giving him high fives like they were doing something. I dug Nick was trying to show me that he had as much game as I did. Country Day was so used to not getting rebounds that as soon as one of them shot the rest of them started going downcourt. I didn't start again but I was in the game during the first half. By the end of the half we were up 32–22 but it wasn't really that close.

Goldy told Ducky he was starting the second half and Ducky looked over at me. I gave him a wink and told him to kick butt. You could tell after two minutes that Ducky didn't want to be out there. He was in the backcourt with Trip and every time Trip passed him the ball he passed it right back or threw it in to Jose, who was playing center.

They set up a play for Ducky where he was supposed to move off a pick at the top of the key and cut across the lane. If everything worked the way it was supposed to, Ducky would be free for a layup. If their center left Jose and cut over and picked Ducky up then he was supposed to dish the ball back over to Jose. Either way we get the layup.

Glen comes out and sets the pick and Ducky ran his man into it like he was supposed to. Jose had moved out from the basket and then turned in toward the hoop, leaving a path for Ducky. Ducky got the pass from Trip and went toward the basket. It was about four steps to the basket and he must have taken three before he realized he hadn't dribbled. He had this pitiful look on his face as the ref blew the whistle and made the signal for traveling.

The guys on the bench cracked up and Ducky looked miserable.

We won the game easy but after the game I found Ducky in the bathroom crying.

"Everybody blows sometimes," I told him.

"I'm quitting the team," he said.

"Why?"

He didn't answer. I put my arm around him just as Nick came in. He saw what was happening and turned around and left right away.

When Ducky finished dressing we walked to the bus stop together. I asked him why he didn't want to play anymore.

"Because I suck," he said.

"You ain't that bad," I lied. "Anyway, if you like doing it, why stop?"

"I'm just messing up the team," he said.

"No, you just don't want to look bad," I said. "But, hey, nothing wrong with that. Nobody wants to go out there and think people are cracking on them. But you got to just go for it, man. You got the heart to back me up against Nick then you got the heart to go out and play ball."

He had his head down and I felt sorry for him. Some other kids came and started talking to us about the game. Light stuff, mostly.

When the bus came I held his sleeve until the other kids got in. "Don't quit the team," I said. "The next time we play I'll get your back. You're going to be okay."

He kind of nodded, but his head was still down.

I was supposed to get over to Mtisha's house to do the homework and I called her just to make sure it was still on. She said I sounded glad to be doing my homework. The truth was I was glad to be seeing her.

First thing I had to do was to get home and get a clean shirt. A guy named Cobby was on the stoop showing off his new puppy and another guy was pretending like he wanted to buy it to feed to his pit bull. I listened to them for a while and then went on upstairs.

"Derek!"

"What?"

"We won today," I said.

"Who you play?"

"Country Day School from Riverdale," I said.

"They any good?" He was talking in this little voice he used when something was wrong.

"Naw." There were some cookies on the table and I took one. "How you doing?"

The water was cold, as usual. I checked out my pop's shaving stuff and copped some of his after-shave lotion. I put a little on my face and some on my chest in case Mtisha was snuggling up or something.

Derek hadn't said anything and I figured he was in a bad mood or something so I left him alone. It was bad enough dealing with Ducky. Maybe I could deal with Derek later.

"You need some money?" I asked him.

He shook his head no.

So there I am with my books, busting over to Mtisha's house feeling like my love had come down over me like butter coming down over popcorn. When I thought about Mtisha I could hook up some pictures of us getting married, going shop-

141

ping in a mall, the whole thing. I wasn't just sweating the chick I was dripping pure unadulterated love.

Got down to where Mtisha lived in a heartbeat. Her mama opened the door and gave me one of those looks that would have killed a little dude.

"Hello, Mr. Harris," she let the words kind of drip out her mouth.

"Good afternoon," I said, sliding by her.

Mtisha's mother was strict but they had a nice pad and a dynamite play room, including a nice stereo with a CD player.

I knocked and Mtisha opened the door. She was wearing white shorts and a soft pink sweater. Sweet as she wanted to be.

We got to the books and she told me to do a problem out loud so she could see how I was doing it.

"I really don't know how to do this one," I said. It looked hard. "That's the same kind of problem they had on the test and you know what I did on that."

"Do the problem," she said.

I looked at it. It was X plus 2 over 5 equals X minus 1 over 2.

"So I looked at it."

"So try it."

"What should I do?"

"Try working it out," she said, sounding like she was getting an attitude.

"What I got to tell you for you to believe I can't do it?"

"You scared of math?" she said. "I mean, like when you go to sleep at night you got to put your math book out the room and lock the door so it won't get you?"

"Don't be messing with me, Mtisha."

"Why are you scared to try it?"

I looked at the problem again. Then I looked at Mtisha. "I thought you wanted to help me?"

"I do," she said. "But I can't help you if you're scared to even try. I'm not going to do it for you. You go on and do it and I'll tell you what you're doing wrong."

"How can I do it when I don't know how?"

"Maybe we can try it another day," she said.

I was watching myself catching an attitude. I was feeling like a fool when I had come over to Mtisha's house feeling good. She was serious so I went on home.

Derek was watching television on the couch and I sat on the other end. We didn't talk, we just sat there and watched some stupid program.

Being mad at Mtisha messed with my mind. No matter what went down I knew she was in my corner, which hurt. Why was I mad at her when she was in my corner like that? But then why did she have to just sit there and make me do the problem?

The books were in the back of the closet where I threw them and I got them out. I looked at the problem again and thought about doing a few things. Maybe I could cross multiply or something. I thought about calling Mtisha and asking her if I should cross multiply, but I didn't want to hear her mouth if she had an attitude.

For supper we had spaghetti and meatballs, which I like. Derek wasn't eating and Moms asked him how he felt and he said depressed.

"What's wrong, honey?"

He mumbled something into his plate which we couldn't hear.

Moms lifted his chin and asked what was wrong again. "You are here with your family, baby," she said.

"What's wrong, boy?" Pops spoke up.

"I lost Slam's video camera."

I just started laughing. You either had to scream and cry or laugh and I started laughing. Then Derek started laughing and I got mad at him for laughing but I couldn't stop laughing.

Moms thought that everybody was going crazy.

"Who got to pay for the video camera?" Pops asked.

"I guess I have to pay for it," I said.

"How did you lose it?" Moms asked Derek.

"I put it down on the stoop and told Darnell to watch it while I went into the store to get some cookies," Derek said. "Then I was looking at the cookies to see which ones I wanted to buy and then I turned around and saw Darnell was there. I asked him who was watching the camera and he said he came to tell me that his mother said he had to go home. So I bought the cookies and then I went back and the camera was gone."

I didn't know what to do. Moms told us to go out and look for the camera, like it might have been a dog or something that would try to find its way back home. What I did was to go down to Carl's.

Carl was my man. People came into his shop to have things fixed, or to buy records or tapes or whatever else he had for sale. Kids bought game cartridges from him or borrowed his tools to fix their bikes. Mostly, though, he dealt with this army of guys who combed the neighborhoods looking through garbage and stuff people had thrown out that might have some value. Then they would line up outside his shop and bring the stuff like they were bringing offerings to a king and he would give them what he thought it was worth.

He also dealt with a bunch of crack heads who sold stuff to help them get the rent, or some food, or just through the day.

"If anybody shows up with a video camera, it's mine," I said.

"That's the camera you had the other day?" he asked.

"Yeah, Derek had it and left it on the stoop."

"Your brother Derek?"

"Yeah. And he didn't even say anything until about three hours after it was gone," I said.

A woman came in and asked about a lamp that Carl had out in front of the store.

"Five dollars," Carl said.

"Does it work?"

"Yeah, I think it works," he said.

"I don't want no lamp that doesn't work," the woman said. "Why don't you check it out for me."

"If I check it out and it works then it's going to be eight dollars," Carl said, messing with the lady.

"How are you going to sell a lamp that doesn't work?" she asked as she started out the door. "You must be out of your head!"

She walked out and down the street.

"Yo, Carl, if you come across the camera, will you look out for me?" I asked.

"Yeah, but if somebody stole it I don't think they'll bring it here," Carl said. "People around here know I don't take stolen stuff. But I'll keep an eye out for it."

"Thanks, man."

When I got back home Moms was having a fit and getting ready to go to the hospital to see Grandma. She was mad at Derek, and at Pops. Her lipstick was smeared and she was close to tears. I was thinking about asking her if she wanted me to go with her, but I didn't want to go.

"Greg, come on and go with me."

"Yes, ma'am."

On the way to the hospital Moms was quiet.

"How's Grandma doing?" I asked.

"Day to day," she answered. "I just feel like she's sinking fast."

"That's what the doctor said?"

"That's what my heart says," Moms said.

We got the train downtown to the hospital and Moms wasn't talking much. We got into the lobby and there was a guy standing there with no shirt on and blood dripping down the front of his chest and onto his stomach and the front of his pants. Two cops had him by the arms, holding them out so he wouldn't bleed on them.

We got up to Grandma's room and she was sitting up eating some ice cream. You could see Moms relax when she saw Grandma looking good. She started talking about how she was doing on her job but Grandma wanted to talk about what she had seen on television. Grandma was looking all right, but you could tell she was still sick.

"How's that thing you making for me?" she asked. "You were supposed to be making a tape of your life."

"It's going good," I said.

"He's really working hard at it, Mama," Moms said.

They went on talking about how television was getting into people's lives and I saw that Moms was talking about anything that Grandma wanted to talk about. I kind of drifted out of the conversation and started thinking about Ice again. The hospital made me think of him. Crack was like being sick, like having AIDS. When you see somebody wasted on crack it even looks like they got AIDS. I wasn't usually scared of AIDS or of crack unless it came near me. I thought I might get messed around with some chick and pick up AIDS, but I wasn't that worried about it because I knew how it spread around. Crack was scarier because I didn't know how it got people.

"Don't you hear your grandmother talking to you, boy?" My mother's voice brought me back.

"Sorry, Grandma. What did you say?"

"I said go out and tell that nurse to bring me some more ice water," Grandma said.

I went out, found the nurse, and asked her to bring Grandma some ice water. I stayed in the hallway for a while, and then Moms came out.

"She wanted to tell me where her jewels were," Moms said. "Go in and say good-bye."

I said good-bye and kissed Grandma. She smoothed my hair back and gave me a real pretty smile.

"Be good to your mama, now," she said.

I thought Moms was right. That Grandma didn't look like she was going to last too long. But on the way home Moms was more cheerful than she had been before. I didn't say nothing to mess up her mood.

At home I drank some milk, snatched up some cookies, and called Mtisha and told her I was sorry. She said I should be which pissed me off. Then I called Ducky.

"You going to play tomorrow?" I asked.

"I don't know," he said.

"You scared of basketball? What you do at night, make sure you put your ball outside so it won't get you?"

"Get out of here."

"See you tomorrow, man."

"Yeah."

CHAPTER TWELVE

Our next game was on Saturday but we all had to go to school first and then take a school bus downtown to Trinity. I liked riding in the bus to the game because it felt good when you showed up and got off the bus and everybody from the other school was looking at you.

Me and Ducky sat in the back. Jimmy sat in front with Goldy and the coach. We had our little band with us, too. Me and Ducky were talking about the football play-offs and wondering if it was going to snow. That's what we were talking about but I was really thinking about what Mtisha had said the day before, that I was scared of math. I didn't think I was scared of math because math couldn't do anything to me. It didn't make sense to be scared of it, but then there was Ducky. Ducky acted like he was scared of basketball. I was ready to run some good doing stuff down on him about it when Nick came on the bus. He saw me in the back of the bus and came to the back.

"How's it going?" Ducky said to him.

"Okay," he said.

"You ready for the game?" Ducky asked.

"I guess so." Nick said to me, "Look, Slam, let me be up front. The coach called me last night and said that a college scout is coming to see me today. I can't look good if you and I aren't playing together."

"A scout from what college?" Ducky asked.

"Brown," Nick said. "Up in Providence."

"Brown?" Ducky looked at me. "They play Ivy League, and they can't even win there."

"I can't afford to go there without a scholarship," Nick said. "I can't afford to go most places with a scholarship."

"Goldy said the Ivy League schools didn't give athletic scholarships," Ducky went on.

"They don't, but if I can play ball for them I know I'll get in," Nick said, looking at me.

"Good luck," I said.

Nick slid out of his seat and went up front. Ducky went back to the conversation about if it was going to snow or not. He was saying that his grandmother had a pain in her hip every time it was going to snow.

My mind drifted to what Nick was saying. The coach had called him and told him that a scout was coming to see him play. How come he wasn't coming to see me play? In a way it hurt, because I could see Nick was getting a chance that I wasn't getting. He was asking me to help him look good to get what I thought I should get.

"Hey! Slam, you awake?" Ducky was talking to me.

"What?"

"What are you thinking about?"

"Nothing, really."

"I was asking you about how your grandmother was," he said. "Didn't you say she was sick?"

"Yeah, she's not doing that good," I said. "My moms doesn't think she's going to make it."

"That's rough."

"Yeah, it is."

We got to Trinity on 91st Street and their cheerleaders were out front. They formed two lines from the bus to the door and cheered us as we went in. That was cool.

Their locker room was old and beat up and their

153

gym wasn't as nice as I thought it was going to be. Before we went out to start the warm-ups the coach said this was going to be our first real test.

"Trinity is one of the schools that has a chance to win the title this year," he said. "They have a good basketball program and some excellent players, players who would start on any high school team in the city. We need to center our game, keep it under control so that if we need to make adjustments we can do it. If we get out there and act like a bunch of cowboys we can't adjust.

"They've got this kid named Brothers who can really play. I'm going to put Slam on him. We're going to play man-to-man as long as it works. On offense I want the ball in Nick's hands as much as possible. I'm moving Trip to forward for quickness and I need everybody to set picks for the guards. This has to be a team effort. Anybody who doesn't play team ball sits down. Now let's go get it done."

Ducky looked over at me. He dug what the coach was really talking about. The whole thing was to make Nick look good.

We started warming up and I checked out the Trinity kids who had come to watch the game. All the guys were dressed in jackets, and ties. Sometimes the ties looked whack but they still had them on. The girls were mostly fine and a lot of them were rich-looking. You could tell by the way their hair was cut just right.

Jimmy came over to me and put his hand out and said something about being sorry for the fight. I shook his hand but I looked away when I did it. He should have said something about punking out when I backed up Ducky, but he didn't.

We lined up for the tip and this guy Brothers lined up with me. He was my height and strong-looking. When I saw that he wore his hair in a ponytail I remembered that Ice had told me about him, that he had a game.

"Sorry I don't have pockets in this uniform," he said.

"What's that mean?" I asked.

"Usually when I come on the court I take a guy's game and put it in my pocket," he said with this crooked grin, "but I had to leave yours in the locker room."

"You got the talk, white boy."

"And I walk the walk, black boy."

"We'll see about that," I said.

Their team was a little shorter than ours, but all of them looked physical. I felt a good kind of nervous, the way I did when I played against the good players in the Rucker Tournaments in Harlem. It was going to be a good game.

They got the tip and Brothers brought the ball down. He came down dribbling the pill between his legs like it was supposed to impress me. I knew as long as it was going between his legs he wasn't going anywhere with it. We got near the top of the key and I moved up on him.

"I'm going right, baby," he said.

"Come on," I answered him.

He dribbled low with his left hand, turned, and put an elbow in my side and ducked his head toward the left. I moved over to cut it off and he spun right and ran me into a pick. I fought through the pick but I was a step behind him. I went up with him, trying to keep my body off him so he wouldn't draw the foul. My eye was dead on the ball as he put it softly against the backboard. They were up by two.

Nick brought the ball down for us. They were slow in getting back and Nick went all the way to the foul line, pulled up, and threw up a jumper to tie the score.

They had two black guys on their team. One was tall and skinny and the other one was short and stocky. The short one, number 5, brought the ball down and passed it in to their center on a simple give-and-go. Number 5 got past Nick but Trip picked him up and partially blocked his shot. The

156

ball came off the boards and Brothers got past me and tapped it back in. Four to two.

Brothers was all over me. When I had the ball he was in my face, and when I didn't have it he kept his hands on me to know where I was and kept his eyes on the ball. Their number 5 could play, too. We started falling behind and the only one on the floor looking good was Brothers. I started thinking about Ice playing him, and figured that Carver would crush these guys.

Nick lost the ball twice bringing it down, and missed two easy jumpers. He wanted to look good but he was looking like nothing, and I wasn't even in the game. The first half went by fast and we were behind 28–16.

"We're doing lousy," Ducky said on the way to the locker room.

"You figure that out on your calculator?" I asked him.

The locker room was quiet. Nobody was saying we were going to lose but that's what everybody was thinking. The coach said that we had to give a hundred and ten percent if we wanted to snatch the game, but he didn't come up with any strategy.

"We're playing a good game, but we need to elevate our effort," he said.

He didn't say anything about me. I had scored

three points in the first half and my man, Brothers, had scored twelve.

We were still feeling bad when we came out for the second half, which made me mad. Us walking with our heads down meant that the guys were convinced we were going to blow. When you think you going to lose you might as well pack up the game bags and get on the bus. What I had was winning at ball, and I took it serious. On the other side Brothers was talking his talk and walking his walk like he owned the world.

Nick come over to me during the warm-ups and asked me if I had any ideas.

"Yeah, I got an idea," I said. "Let's win."

"How?"

"Give me the ball," I said.

"You got it," he said.

The team huddled and put our fists together.

"Let's put some muscle in the hustle," Trip said.

"And let's get the ball to Slam," Nick said.

Jimmy shot him a look and Nick stared him down.

Okay. So it was show time or blow time. We got the tap and Nick brought the ball down. I took Brothers to the baseline and got under the boards. He had expected me to move back outside and when he saw I was trying to position him he leaned on me good. He knew the game. Nick shook his man at the foul circle and drove the right side of the lane. Their center moved over to cut him off and Nick passed off to me. A fake took Brothers into the air and I went up a split second later, leaned into him for the foul and put the ball against the boards.

The whistle blew and when I looked the ref was pointing to Brothers for the foul. My foul shot rimmed the basket and fell in.

Brothers brought the ball down for them, dribbling the ball between his legs the same way he had before. I was looking around for the pick when he passed the ball into the center. Brothers put his hand on my chest and just pushed a little. I went to slap his hand away and he cut past me toward the hoop. He got the handoff from their center, went up and drove through the dunk. Their crowd went into a wild, crazy-butt chant.

We had the ball and I went coast-to-coast with Brothers breathing on me. I decided to just power over him but he went up with me and slapped my stuff away. It went out over my head and when I turned I saw that Nick had it for a split second. Then it was back to me and I was going up again. This time I got over Brothers and made the deuce.

It was our deuce but Brothers was getting to me

and he knew it. Every time I looked at him he was smiling. Their center lost the ball the next time down and we got back faster than they did for another deuce. Trinity was strong, but they couldn't run that good.

They brought it down slow and Brothers pointed at me and started waving to his team. He wanted them to clear out so he could go one-on-one with me. I pushed up on him and kept a hand on his hip. He kept his body between me and the ball and kept an elbow in my chest. He rocked back and forth a little, faking a move to his left and running his mouth.

"What you want me to do, man?" he said. "Your choice."

"Shut up!" I said, and I was sorry I said it because I didn't want him to know I didn't dig his rap.

He made another fake left and I felt a hand in the small of my back. I reached behind me, looking for the pick, when he took off. Second slam.

Trip threw up a shot for us and it was blocked but Jimmy got it and bounced it to me. I went down the right side with Brothers almost in my skin. Nick was curling on the baseline. On the way up for the shot I saw that Brothers had his arms up in my way and I brought the ball back down and around my back to where I hoped Nick was. Nick made the basket.

Their number 5 took the ball out, threw it into Brothers, and he spun around with a big step and ran smack into Trip for a charging foul. That was Brother's third foul and they called a time-out. The scoreboard said Visitor's 27, Home 32.

"Slam, he's doing everything on that first step," Ducky said as I sat down. "He's got that one real long step."

We had been twelve points down at the half and now we were only five down with the ball.

When play started again we inbounded the ball on the side and I took it at the top of the key.

"Come on!" Brothers beckoned me to him.

I went right up with the three-pointer and it didn't touch nothing but net.

They threw a long pass that went out of bounds and we got the ball. We brought it down and Jimmy put the ball up. It bounced around the rim and he got it and put it back up again. It bounced off again and I got it and put it up. It bounced off again and their tall black guy went up for it. The pill bounced off his hands and went against the backboard and in. The score was tied.

Ducky was right. What Trinity was doing was

setting things up for Brothers. All he needed was a heartbeat for that one quick step and he was gone. Once he got past he had a strong move to the hoop. I moved up on him and kept slapping at the ball so he had to keep his back to me. That slowed down that big step. And I told Jimmy to yell out when I was moving toward a pick so I wouldn't have to reach for it.

We were playing them good and you could tell that the team was getting their confidence back.

I was looking for the chance to slam on Brothers and it came with a minute and a half left and us up by three. Glen was in the game and he picked off a pass that was headed for their center. I broke and Glen threw the ball downcourt. The ball arrived six feet in front of our foul line just as I was crossing it. I grabbed the ball and went up with Brothers all over me. But I was definitely flying. I brought it down with two hands as hard as I could and heard it rip through the net. We were up by five.

"How you like it?" I asked Brothers as we come down the court. He didn't say nothing.

They brought the ball up slow, confident, and Brothers took me in deep. I fronted him and he went out to the corner. He got the ball there and I cut off the baseline but he wasn't going anyplace. He just popped the three from the corner and we were only up two with a whole minute to play.

The coach was signaling for us to take some time off the clock. We ran it down for a while waiting for them to foul us.

"Foul nine!" Brothers was calling when number 9, Trip, got the ball.

The black guy on their team ran over toward Trip with his hands out like he was going to foul him then slapped the ball away. He took off after the ball and I took off after him. I caught up with him halfway down the lane and he dished out to Brothers in the corner.

Bam! The dude hit his second three in a row. We were down by one with eight seconds to play.

We called a time-out and the coach set up a play for me.

"Two picks. I want Jimmy at high post and Glen at low post," he said. "Nick's got the ball. Slam, you start baseline and run and come out to the lane. Try to run your man into either the low pick or the high pick. It's got to go bang-bang because we only have eight seconds left. If there's any problem inbounding, call another time-out, we have one left. Nick, if Slam goes in you come out for the dish in case he gets tied up, if he's making a move on the outside you go deep. Jimmy clear out the paint. Now, put your hands together."

It sounded on the money. We put our hands together and went out for the last play.

Jose was in and he was inbounding. Trinity had Brothers on me, as usual. I checked his mug and he wasn't smiling. The ball came in and I ran along the baseline and past Glen with Brothers on my hip. I moved him into Jimmy at the high post but Brothers got past him, too.

I turned and headed back toward the hoop as Nick got the pill. Nick went up in the air and one of their players went up with him. He brought the ball toward me and Brothers cut me off as the guy guarding him brought his hand down to stop the pass. Nick twisted in the air and somehow got the ball against the backboard. Yes! Yes!

The gym was going wild and I looked up and saw that time had run out. We had won! Our bench was going crazy.

Then I looked over and saw that the coach had his head to his hands. I turned and looked at the ref and he was signaling no basket.

"Time had run out!" he said.

I looked for Nick and then for the coach. I

turned back toward the refs but they were already headed for the locker room.

Some of the players from Trinity were coming over to shake our hands. Nick walked away without shaking anybody's hand and the rest of us followed.

CHAPTER THIRTEEN

We didn't shower, just got on the bus smelling funky and feeling worse. Coach went around saying that we had made a strong comeback and telling everybody not to feel bad. He was feeling bad, though, and you could see that all over his face.

They made us go all the way back to the school and then the coach told us we still had a chance to win, because Trinity had lost to Hunter and they still had to face Carver. What he didn't say was that we had to face Hunter and Carver, too.

The coach who had come to see Nick play was at the school and he talked with Goldy for a while before he left. I asked Goldy if he said anything about the game.

"Said you guys looked pretty good once you got your game together," Goldy said.

"What did you think?" I asked.

166

"I think it doesn't matter," Goldy said. "It's over now. We have to go on to the next game."

Yeah. Me and Ducky started to the bus stop and a car pulled up. It was Ducky's mom.

"Can we drop you someplace?" she asked.

"Bet."

Yo, Ducky's mom was fine. If she wasn't white and about thirty-something I might have given her a play. She got the hint real quick that we had blown the game and went on about how crowded it was downtown. Ducky didn't want to hear that mess and neither did I so she shut up.

"I'll come to the next game if I can," she said when she left me off on 145th.

"You lucky?" I asked.

"I think so," she said, and flashed me a pretty smile.

I got upstairs and a little big-eyed boy named Donnie was standing on the landing.

"Your father got shot," he said.

I busted down the hall and saw the door was unlocked. My heart was jumping when I ran in. Moms was making coffee at the stove and Derek was reading a comic.

"Where's Pops?" I asked.

"He's in the living room watching television," Moms said. "You hear he broke his arm?"

"Broke his arm?" I looked down the hallway toward the living room but I couldn't see nothing. "Donnie said he got shot."

"He's only four," Moms said. "Anytime somebody gets hurt around here the little kids think they got shot. No, he just broke his arm."

"How he break it?"

"We were shopping on Eighth Avenue and he stepped on a newspaper that somebody had put over some oil and slipped on it," Moms said. "Cried like a baby."

"Get out of here."

"Yes he did." Moms was smiling. "Laid right on that sidewalk and cried. Been acting like a baby ever since."

I went into the living room and Pops was watching a talk show. He had a cast on his arm and he was looking beat up.

"I broke my arm," he said.

"Sorry to hear that," I said. "You want me to do anything for you?"

"No, just ask your mama to come in for a minute."

I went on out to the kitchen and told Moms what he said. She shook her head and went toward the living room.

Losing the game against Trinity was whack. The thing was that Brothers got my game. We had a comeback but during the whole first part of the game I was playing weak. When a dude gets your game that strong he should be a lot better than you and Brothers wasn't all that, and I knew it. Or maybe he was and I didn't want to admit that a white boy had done the thing to me.

The phone rang and I could hear Derek going for it. He only had two friends that call him but he likes answering the phone. He come to the door and said that it was Mtisha.

Mtisha asked me what I was doing.

"Chillin'."

"I heard you lost against Trinity."

"Dang! Who told you?"

"Marcus. You know that guy lives over near the car wash?" Mtisha said. "Got a mountain bike?"

"He told you?"

"Yep. Anyway, I'm going to Sam's for dinner because my mother is going to a church meeting," Mtisha said. "You want to come? It's on me."

"Yeah."

I was hoping she wasn't going to try to cheer me up because we lost the game. People who ain't into ball don't even know what it means to lose.

The whole name of Sam's is Sam's Fish Box which is a stupid name. Maybe if you're a West Indian and like to eat stuff that burns your mouth out it's okay, but I don't dig it. They make nice chicken, which is the best thing they make, and also a pretty good curried goat. But I don't like the goat because the bones are too small and you could be eating a dog or something. Also, Sam don't know how to talk to people. I don't like people cracking on me.

It was cold out and Sam had all those big pots on and the windows were steamed up. Mtisha was sitting in the back and I went over and gave her a little kiss. She smelled good.

"So what's happening?" I saw she had a math book on the chair next to her.

"Nothing much, what do you want to eat?"

"Something light," I said. "Maybe some chicken and some red beans."

Sam came over before I got my butt on the seat. He was broad and brown-skinned, and the sweat was dripping off his forehead. He asked me what I wanted.

"Give me a minute, man," I said.

"You ain't got no money," Sam said to me. "What you need a whole minute for?"

"How you know I ain't got money. I could be fat."

"Your ears too small to have any money," Sam said. "You see them millionaires? They got them big ears. Anytime a dollar rustle they hear it. Them small ears you got, all you can hear is pennies falling."

"You got chicken?"

"I got catfish and whitings," Sam said. "Which one you want?"

"Get the whitings," Mtisha said. "Catfish look nasty."

"Okay, give me the whitings," I said.

Sam went on back to his pots. Mtisha was having some kind of stew and tea with lemon. You didn't sit in Sam's and not spend some money. You didn't sit there all day, either.

"You smell like peaches or something," I said. "Or is that just love I'm sniffing?"

"That's Sam's curry you smelling," she said. "You talk to Ice yet?"

"No, I was planning to talk to him Monday after school," I lied. "What you got the books for?"

"I got this idea," she said, pulling out a notebook. "I'm going to give you a whole lot of problems to do so I can tell just where you need help."

She handed me the notebook and I opened it. She had actually written out 60 problems. "You kidding, right?"

"You see a smile on my face?"

"It'll take me forever to get all this done."

"That's okay," Mtisha said. "I'm young."

Yeah.

Sam brought the fish and it looked terrible. Mtisha poked at it with her finger.

"That looks like the catfish," she said.

"That ain't the catfish," Sam said. "That's the whiting. You don't know catfish when you see it?"

"Taste it," Mtisha said.

I tasted it and it didn't taste too bad and I said I'd eat it. But when I looked up at Sam he was smiling. It was just like him to give me the catfish and make believe it was the whiting. Jive turkey.

On Sunday afternoon I sat with Pops a while and we had a light rap. We don't talk all that much because he don't have a lot to say. He can't tell me how to play ball 'cause he don't play ball. He can't tell me how to deal with the streets because I already learned that on my own. He can't tell me much about how to get over because he ain't got over. I like to rap with him, though, especially when he tells me stuff he did as a kid. It sounded lame, but it was interesting because I know how his program turned out. One time he said he thought buzzards was circling over his head waiting for him to get weak enough to fall. When he was first saying it I didn't like it because I thought maybe he was seeing things but now I was seventeen I was beginning to understand what he was talking about.

"What you going to do about the video camera?" he asked.

"Maybe it'll show up," I said.

"And if it don't?"

"I'll just have to tell them at school," I said.

He nodded. I knew he didn't have the money to pay for it.

"So what you thinking about that guy coming around helping you with your math?" he asked.

"You know Mtisha?"

"Your girl?"

"Sort of my girl," I said. "She's really good at math and she's helping me. I think it's going to be cool."

"You don't need the guy?"

"Uh-uh."

"Yeah, that's good," he said.

He nodded to himself, and I thought he looked relieved. I was relieved, too.

"What you mean 'sort of' your girl?" he asked. "I thought you had her sewn up? You don't know how to deal with women?"

"Hey, you can't really tell me nothing about no women," I said. "And don't tell me you were some kind of nickel-and-dime Romeo, either."

"I got your Mama," he said.

"Don't even go there, man."

Monday morning came and it looked like it wanted to snow but it didn't, just got cold as anything. I met Ducky in the hallway at Latimer and I told him how fine his mama looked.

"She's been fixing herself up since they separated," he said.

"Your parents separated?"

"I don't think it's permanent," Ducky said, unwinding this enormous scarf from around his neck. "When they were arguing she was really screaming at him but after he left she was crying all over the place."

"Where did you get that scarf?"

"I saw one like this in a movie and this guy was getting all the girls," Ducky said.

"You getting all the girls?"

"Yeah, every time I go up and jam another girl

174

calls me up and wants to give me her true love," he said.

I wanted to ask him if he thought the guys in the NBA really got as many chicks as they say in the papers but then Mr. Parrish called me over.

"I saw your tape," he said.

"Yeah, I thought maybe I'd do something else," I said.

"Margie came on with an immature attitude when she brought me the tape," Mr. Parrish said. "Is that why you don't want to go on with it?"

"No, it's just boring," I said.

"Look, I think you have something good going on in your tape. I'd like to see you do about three hours more and then cut it down so that it says what you want it to say. There's a statewide arts contest and I'd like to enter your tape. I don't know how good it'll do, naturally, but I think it might have a chance."

"You think it's okay?"

"You see well," Mr. Parrish said. "And you have a feel for your neighborhood that Margie doesn't. Think about it."

"Yeah, okay."

That made me feel good for about two whole minutes while I was thinking about myself as a big-deal moviemaker. Then I remembered that I had lost the camera.

We had practice and Trip's father is there. He can't see the games or the practice, but he shows up. I could dig it.

The practice went all right. We ran some four-on-five plays to learn how to avoid traps. I had never done that before and it was all right. Then we did some wind sprints and finally had a half hour of just shooting practice. Nick said that he got a letter from the athletic department at Brown.

"What did it say?"

"They said they would like me to consider Brown," he said. He had this big smile on his face.

"Hey, congratulations," I said.

Definitely a raggedy situation. My game was stronger than Nick's but the guy from Brown only had eyes for him. Nobody was talking about me. While I was in the shower I thought about it a lot. Nick had good grades and he had a nice look about him and everything. Or maybe it was just because he was white, I didn't know. Ducky said that Brown didn't have a good team. It didn't make me no never mind. I was down with any school that wanted me to come and play ball.

Most of the guys were gone when I got out of the shower, but Goldy was there.

"Yo, Goldy, can I ask you a question?"

"Go ahead."

"Nick said that he got a letter from the coach at Brown," I said. "How come nobody's interested in my game? You think it's because I'm black?"

"Could be," Goldy said. "And it could be because Nick has better grades, or that he did well in the PSAT, or because Brown doesn't think they can get anybody with your talents."

"Yeah. Could be," I said. "Let me ask you another question. You think I got a chance to play college ball?"

"You're the one who has to figure that out," Goldy said, tossing towels in the laundry bin. "You have to figure out how well you're doing."

"But say I was your blood, right?" I straddled the bench near Goldy. "What would you say? Would you say I got a shot?"

"If you were my blood?" Goldy leaned against the wall. "You mean, like, if you were my son or something?"

"Yeah, what would you say?"

"I'd tell you like my father told me," Goldy said. "He went through a lot of hell during the Second World War. At first he was bitter, then he was mad, then he figured it all out. That's what he told me, that he had figured it all out. What he said was that the only thing that mattered was how well you did what you loved. You know what I mean?

"If science is your life, then you got to love science and do science with everything you have. If basketball is what you're about then that's what you got to do. You have to keep your eyes open and see what's going on around you, of course. But what you do you got to do it to the max. You know what I mean?"

"It don't work like that, Goldy," I said. "I see people busting their tails every day and they ain't going no place."

"They're not doing what they love, Slam," Goldy said. "For whatever reason we don't always have the chance to do what we love. That's a special gift from God. But when you are doing what you love, you got to bust it. And when you do, it works. I can't tell you how it works, but it works."

CHAPTER FOURTEEN

Ice lived on 141st Street, which used to be one of the best blocks in the hood. Then the corner of the building he lived in fell off. Square business. The whole corner just fell off. People were lying in their beds and when that corner fell off they fell out the building. The collapse killed three people. Nobody in Ice's family got killed but they were shook up bad.

His family moved in with an aunt that lived across the street and that's where I went to talk to him. He wasn't home but his mother was there. Ice's mom used to be like my second mother. When we were small every time she bought something for Ice she bought the same thing for me. Then Ice's father got stabbed to death on the same day that Showman's bar had a fire. His mother got real religious after that.

"What you doing with yourself these days, boy?" Ice's mom was dark-skinned and slight. She was washing the floor as she talked, making patterns of soapy water on the linoleum.

"Going to school, playing a little ball, taking care of business," I said.

"Hope you leaving the girls alone," she said.

"I'm trying to leave them alone," I said. "But you know how that is."

"Don't you go out here and make no babies," she said, wringing out the mop. "Worse thing a young boy can do for himself is go around making a lot of babies."

"Ice been home?"

"He was home about four or so," she said. "I can't wait until we get our own place again. Ice don't feel comfortable here. And you know he having trouble with that girlfriend of his. I don't know what he sees in her anyway."

"I know what he sees in her," I said. "She's fine."

"There's more to life than being fine," Mrs. Reese said. "That ammonia bother you?"

"Not that much," I lied. "You put your hands in that stuff?"

"No, but this woman's floors need something," Mrs. Reese said. "They had this old dog that couldn't get around much before he died. These floors stink something terrible when the heat comes up."

"Yeah. Look, tell Ice I was by," I said, putting my coat on.

"Okay," she said.

"You want anything to eat before you go?" she said when we had reached the door.

"No, I'm good."

"Slam, you got a girlfriend too?" she asked.

"Yeah," I said. "We're pretty tight."

"Just remember you got plenty of time," she said. "Don't be in no hurry."

"Yes, ma'am."

When I got downstairs Ice was on the stoop with Willie King. Willie used to have a heavy game. He could really get up. Two years ago he went to the Knicks camp and rocked with their starting five. Then he got busted and had to do a half a calendar on Rikers Island. When he got out of jail he was different. Some guys said that he had been turned out. Every time I looked at him and thought about him being turned out, being raped by other dudes, I felt bad for him.

"What's happening?" I said.

"Ballplayer!" Willie put up his hand and I slapped him five.

"What's going on?" Ice was clean. He was wearing a black overcoat, gray suit, yellow silk shirt, and gray suede kicks.

"You look like you going to Hollywood," I said.

"Same thing I told him," Willie said. "He's going to have to start handing out tickets to all the babes. Make them wait in line."

"Heard you lost to Trinity," Ice said.

"Man, nobody in Harlem even know about Trinity until we lost that game," I said. "Now everybody and their mama knows about them."

"How you let a bunch of preppie boys beat you?" Ice asked. "You should go hide your face."

"They jumped out quick and got a little lead and we had to struggle to make a comeback," I said. "At the end we were down by a point and our guy made the last shot but the refs said he got it off after the buzzer."

"They got them a white boy that thinks he's Larry Bird." Ice looked sideways at Willie. "He talks trash but he can back it up pretty good."

"Yeah, he talked a lot," I said. "If I play him again I'll have to deal with him personally."

"I hear you," Willie said. "I got to be moving now but the next time you play let me know. Ice said you had a sweet game."

"I'll let you know," I said.

Willie went down the street and cut into the park. Ice kept talking about how good Willie used to be when he played down at Riverside Church.

"Nobody could mess with him," Ice said. "You just had to keep the ball away from him. We played against him when he was with the Gauchos and you know how we beat him?"

"How?"

"We found the worse guy on their team and didn't guard him," Ice said. "We let the guy just run free. Willie kept feeding the guy the ball and he couldn't make a shot. Guy threw up so many bricks he could have been in construction. He scored nine points the whole game and we kept Willie to twelve."

I watched Willie walk through a crowd of kids. Being good on the court hadn't helped him at all. The wind seemed to pick up a little and I pulled my coat shut against the cold and pushed my mind away from Willie.

"Yo, man, how come we don't hang out no more?" I said. "We used to hang out big time. Now you're always on the run."

"Hey, got to be doing that juggling thing," Ice said. He was looking across the street where there was a small crowd gathered over something on the ground. "Between going to school, playing ball, and trying to get paid once in a while the time gets away."

"You look like you getting paid heavy," I said. "You dressing like you ready to make the cover of some magazine."

"When they let you in the FBI?"

"What's that supposed to mean?"

"You checking out my closet, figuring out how much I get paid, you must be FBI or something," Ice said.

"No big thing."

Across the street the crowd was getting bigger and Ice pointed to it and started off the stoop. I went after him.

The guy laying on the sidewalk was about forty or something. He was big but a little flabby-looking. The way he was puffing, it looked like he was having trouble getting enough air. Every time he gasped there would be a little puff of steam like coming from his mouth. His eyes were open but they were rolling back and forth real quick.

"Guy's having a heart attack," Ice said. "Yo, anybody call nine-one-one?"

"Yeah, I called," a pretty, light-skinned woman in glasses said. "'Bout five minutes ago."

"Go call them again," Ice said. "Tell them it's a heart attack."

Ice pulled out a roll of bills from his pocket and gave the woman twenty dollars. She looked at it, looked at Ice, then turned and headed to the phone.

"Anybody know CPR?" Ice held up another twenty.

Two dudes dropped down to the ground and went for the guy's mouth. The guy that got there first started giving him mouth-to-mouth and the other guy started pushing on his chest. I don't know if they were doing it right, but the brothers were definitely working.

I was looking down but I saw Ice glance over at me. He didn't stay on me, just looked at me for a moment to see if I was checking him out.

The emergency service ambulance and the cops arrived at the same time. The emergency guys already had their rubber gloves on when they got to the dude. First they checked his eyes to see if he was overdosing, then they listened to his heart.

"He having a heart attack?" the woman who had called 9-1-1 asked.

"Looks like it," the emergency attendant said.

"That's what he said," the woman said.

The cops were still sitting in their car and one of

them called over an emergency guy to see what was happening. Then they split.

Ice gave the guys who had given the man CPR twenty dollars each. We went back to the stoop as they got the guy in the ambulance.

"That was real tough," I said. "You took charge of the deal."

"No big thing," Ice said.

Two old women came down the street. They were arm in arm and they looked like they liked each other. I like to see old people hanging out together. When I see them I think about all the times they must have had and all the things they must have seen.

"You know, I was worried about you for a while," I said. I was tense as I talked, almost holding my breath. "I thought you were dealing."

"Bianca tell you that?"

"I think she was worried about it."

"Woman stays on my nerves, man." Ice shook his head like he was disgusted. "I got a little light gig I'm trying to build into something and she talking like a stone lame. Maybe she wants me to deal."

"Ain't nobody want you to deal," I said. "Just trying to look out for a homey."

"How I'm going to blow with all my people around me?" Ice smiled.

"I hear you."

"Look, I'm not funny or nothing, but I know when I feel some real love around me." Ice came over to me and hugged me. Then he said he had to get upstairs and find something to eat.

On the way home I felt good and bad. I was telling myself how good it was that Ice had got the woman to call 9-1-1 again and how he had paid the brothers to give the heart attack dude CPR.

What I said and what I should have said ran through my mind and it was all weak. Me and Ice were edging in on a truth and we both knew it. That was what he was really saying when he said he loved me and when we hugged.

The thing was I didn't see nothing in Ice that I didn't see in me or Pops. Sometimes it was like we were all edging around that big truth we knew was out there waiting to get us. That's why we could hang tough when we hung together, and why when things broke down and one brother or sister showed wrong we came down so hard. The same truth that got your brother in the middle of the block was waiting for you on the corner.

When I got home my moms and pops had been fighting. No big thing. I didn't even have to ask if they were fighting about money. They never talked about money, but that's what the fight was always about. They were in the kitchen working hard at ignoring each other, which was always a trip. Moms was washing some collard greens in the sink and Pops was sitting at the kitchen table reading the newspaper. He had liquor on his breath. I know he didn't want to hear her mouth but he wasn't going to go slinking into the bedroom.

"What you think about getting a television in the bedroom?" Moms said to me.

"Whatever."

"'Whatever'?" She had her hand on her hip. "What's that supposed to mean?"

"It don't mean nothing," I said. "You ask me what I thought about getting a television in the bedroom and I don't care, that's all."

"I just asked your opinion, Mr. Harris."

"I don't have an opinion," I said.

"Well, I don't see why, if I'm out here working every day, I can't have a television in the bedroom so I can watch my programs in the evenings," Moms said. "I just don't know why. Maybe I'm not good enough to have a television."

Pops was turning the page as I headed for my bedroom.

"Mtisha called," he said. His voice was blurry from the booze.

I laid on the bed and thought about calling Mtisha. Then I thought what it would be like to be married to her. She'd probably want a whole lot of stuff. Once, just before New Year's, I went with her to the Pioneer market to get some dried black-eyed peas for Hopping John and we were talking about what we wanted to do. Mostly dream stuff. I was talking about getting my picture on a box of cereal. She said she wanted a boat.

I couldn't see myself buying a boat or even traveling anyplace on a boat. It wasn't because I couldn't swim either.

When I called Mtisha's house her mom answered. She told me Mtisha had a surprise for me.

"You don't deserve a good girl like Mtisha," Mrs. Clark said. There was a smile in her voice. "Next thing I know she'll be cooking for you. You know she can cook, don't you?"

"Mtisha? No, I didn't know she could cook."

"You tell her to make dinner for you some night," Mrs. Clark said. "Here she is now."

"Hello, Slam?"

"Yeah, I heard you could cook."

"I can, but guess what I got?"

"What?"

"Guess!"

"How I know what you got?"

"Guess!"

"You got a scholarship to some college?"

"The video camera," she said. "A guy sold it to Carl for a dime and he remembered you saying you lost it. He gave it to me but you got to drop by his place with the dime."

"Hey, I'll come right over to pick it up," I said.

"Uh-uh. I told Carl you were going to bring his ten dollars over today, so you do that," Mtisha said. "I'm going downtown with my mother. You can pick the camera up tomorrow."

"Yeah? Look, Carver is playing Trinity tomorrow. Bring the camera to the game and I'll meet you there," I said. "And don't lose it before I get there."

"How did the talk with Ice go?"

"I don't know," I said. "I kept looking around for something to say that wasn't old."

"Is he dealing?"

"I don't know," I said. "He says he's not."

"You believe him?"

"Yeah, I guess so," I said.

"You should know if he's telling the truth," she said.

"Yeah, I believe him."

"Get to Carl's," she said.

CHAPTER FIFTEEN

Man, I loved me some Carver. When I showed up at my old school everybody knew me. Two guys who hung out together, Big Tony and Ouzi Smith, started yelling out that I was a scout and they should put me out. I dug it.

I got this move on. When I spotted Mtisha I came up behind her, put my arm around, and when she turned to see who it was I planted one right on her lips. She gave me a look like she was mad but I know she dug it.

"You give Carl his money?" she asked.

"Yeah. I got it from my pops."

"Carl looks out," she said.

"He was as happy to find the camera for us as I was to get it back," I said.

"He tell you a crack head brought it in?"

"No," I answered.

"You didn't want to know, did you?" she asked, suddenly serious.

"I guess I didn't," I said. She didn't answer, just nodded.

We started making our way through the crowd into the fold-down wooden stands. Carver's band was at mid-court so we sat down from them so we could hear ourselves.

"Yo, Slam, you here to see us tear up these white boys?" It was Abdul, a guy from the block. He was wearing a Raiders jacket and a hood.

"Yo, Abdul, what's happening?" Abdul used to play ball, nothing heavy, but he had some game until he dropped out of school.

"How come you ain't down there on the court, man?" Abdul said, knowing that I didn't go to Carver anymore.

"I'm just here checking everything out," I said.

The Carver band played "The Star-Spangled Banner" and everybody stood up, then they broke into "Lift Every Voice," and I saw that everybody from Trinity stayed standing along with the black kids from Carver. Down on the floor I saw Ice in the maroon-and-yellow warm-up suit that Carver wore. He was looking good.

When the game started I was nervous. Mtisha

192

said I should tape the game and I said yes, but I was so nervous she even noticed it.

"What's wrong with you?" she asked.

"I guess it was that kiss," I said. "You know you mess with my soul, don't you?"

She give me a look like she was searching my face looking for the real me. I gave her a light kiss. Yes! That was the RIGHT move. She kind of sighed and I know her love was coming down. It almost made me forget how nervous I was.

The thing was, I didn't want Brothers, the dude with the ponytail from Trinity, to do the thing to my man Ice. On the other hand, I didn't want Ice to really tear up Brothers. If I couldn't tear him up I didn't want Ice to do it, either.

Ice did it. Ice came out smoking. It was tap and rap because I saw him start to run his mouth from the get-go. The whole first half was Carver, and everybody in the stands was going crazy. On one play Ice pulled that little move that the dude from St. John's always did. He came down the court, broke near the foul line, dipped his knees and came up without ever leaving the ground. Brothers went up in the air and Ice went around him for a reverse slam.

Ice moved smoothly around the floor, thin legs

wide apart, head bobbing, the ball moving from his hand to the floor and rushing back to his light palms as if it was a giant yo-yo. He could pass with a single movement, a sweep of his arm would send the ball through a crowd of straining bodies to just the right outstretched hands, just the right player.

It was the thing with Ice, you could never tell what he was going to do. There was no getting-ready move, no need for him to make three moves to set you up. He would be coming down the right side and move a half-step faster or a half-step slower and you would think, or drop a hand, or move a knee, and then Ice would be in the air, the ball poised on his fingertips, the wrist bent back, and whatever you did would be too late.

Trinity, against Carver, was all huff and puff. Brothers got a breakaway jam and made some nice passes but at the end of the first half it was Carver 34 and Trinity 20.

The Carver cheerleaders were on one side during the halftime break and the Trinity cheerleaders were on the other side. They took turns and every time Carver did something all the kids from Carver, which was most of the people there, cheered. When Trinity's cheerleaders did their thing everybody booed. Mtisha taped that.

The second half started out the same way as the

first half ended. Carver got the pill, busted it down-court, and Carver's shooting guard threw it up for Ice. Ice put his palm on it and slammed it through.

Okay, then Trinity get the ball and Brothers brings it down. He stops at the top of the key and tells his team to clear out. Everybody cracks on this and the whole Carver team moves away and it's just Brothers and Ice working the show. Brothers makes a little okeydokey move and Ice goes around him for the pill. But then Brothers pulls the pill in and he's clear for the basket, but instead of going for the basket he comes out again and around Ice. He turns Ice and then he drives in slow. Ice is a half-step behind him at the foul line but two steps in and he's dead on the dude. Brothers goes up real strong and I expect Ice to throw away his stuff but it don't happen. It just don't happen and Brothers slams again.

That gave the whole Trinity team some juice and they made a little light comeback but then Carver put the game away. Ice didn't do anything great in the second half, but then he didn't have to, the game was really over in the first half. Some-times I thought Ice looked tired, sometimes I thought he just didn't care what Brothers had done. He had already beat him and that's what counted. It was dope checking out the scene through the viewfinder. There were a lot of things you couldn't see when you had your eye up to the camera, but there were a lot of things you could see better because you were concentrating on them.

All in all Ice was the man, but Brothers had that one play on him.

After the game Mtisha was talking about Ice and how well he had played. She was going on about how he had did this and did that, stuff that he hadn't even done. I knew she was just glad to see him do well.

I took Mtisha home and tried to figure out my next move. That gentle kiss was a nice move and I thought I could get in another one and then throw something heavy at her. Especially if I could get her on her mama's couch.

"So maybe I'll see you tomorrow," she said, in front of her apartment building.

"Thought I'd come up for a while," I said.

"Capital N, small o," she said. "That spells No."

"You mean you just want me to go home when my heart is all filled up with love for you?"

"That works."

"How come every time I talk to you I feel like my mouth is too small to get the words out?" I asked her.

"How come every time I talk to you I feel my mouth is too big?" she said. "And I got to watch what comes out?"

"What you afraid of saying?" I asked.

"You can't figure it out?" she flashed that famous smile, white teeth in the prettiest black face in Harlem, and disappeared into her hallway leaving me on the stoop.

No, I couldn't figure it out. All the way home I thought about what she was afraid of saying. Maybe she didn't want to say she loved me. No, that wasn't it. She wasn't that shy. She had said she loved me before. She would always say it in a half-kidding way, but she had said it.

It could have been something about sex. That's what I figured it had to be about. Mtisha wasn't the kind of girl that just fell down because you took her out for Chinese food. But maybe she was getting nervous around me. That's what I figured was on her mind. Even if it wasn't, that was what was on my mind so I let it be on hers, too.

CHAPTER SIXTEEN

When I got home I showed Derek the camera and he busted out a smile that was something else. He started running down how sorry he was that he had lost it. I had thought about what I was going to say to him but I let him slide.

"I know you're not going to let me use it again," he said.

"No, you can use it," I said. "But you lose the sucker again I'm going to put out a serious contract on your life."

"No, if I lose it I'm going to put out a serious contract out on me and then I'm going to hire myself to bump me off," he said.

He kept on talking about how careful he was going to be and what he was going to do to anybody who tried to take the camera from him. I was looking at him and I saw that he was getting to be kind of good-looking. The mirror was right behind him and I checked him out against me and he wasn't that bad. It didn't really matter because I was still going to get all the babes.

After we had turned out the lights he came over to my bed and rubbed my shoulder the way he used to do when he was scared to be in the dark. It was good to have a little brother.

In school we got our P.S.A.T. scores back. They had them separated into classes and Mr. Tate, looking like a stuffed sausage with a tie, came to the class to give them out. First he had to give his talk.

"Nobody knows you outside of your immediate friends and family," he said. "So they look for markers to give them a clue to just who you are. Are you a decent person? They look to see if you have a discipline record. They ask your teachers for recommendations. Are you a person who does his work in school? They look for your grades. Are you college material? They look at all these things and then add the S.A.T. to it.

"I'm not telling you anything you don't know. I want you to look at your S.A.T. scores and think what it means to people on the admissions boards in these colleges. This is the P.S.A.T. and you have a chance to improve your scores with some study and practice."

He handed out the scores, which is really like a form you have to tear apart. The kids who knew they did good started ripping theirs open right away. I slid mine in my notebook.

On television they had these two guys who were trying to get a basketball scholarship and one of them couldn't get 700 on the S.A.T. The guy had an all right game but it wasn't bodacious. He was a player, but he was up at forward when he didn't have the weight to be no forward. Anyway, he had to go to a junior college. Then, on this same program, this black newscaster came on and said that any idiot could get 700.

I figure that the kid who didn't get the 700 was somewhere listening to the whole thing. The newscaster didn't show the kid any respect at all. If the kid had busted a cap in the newscaster's heart everybody would have said the kid was wrong. The diss was cool, but the comeback was wrong.

I went to the bathroom and sat in the john near the door. Somebody was smoking weed in the booth near the window.

Some of the scores I heard in the classroom and in the halls were real high. Trip got a 1200 and change and Tony Fornay got 1100. My scores were low, but I added them up and they came up to 740.

They weren't kicking no butt, but if somebody wanted to offer me a scholarship I could take it. That was before Mtisha started helping me with the math, too.

Hunter was the next game and I knew I had to get up for it. Getting the 740 on the S.A.T. was going to let me take a basketball scholarship. Now I had to go out and get one.

The game was held at Hunter College and I dug that. The gym was dynamite with glass backboards that came down from the ceiling. The locker room had rubdown benches, a whirlpool, and a weight room off to one side. Ducky liked the first-aid cabinet. It was locked but Ducky said it was so big they could probably do brain surgery in the locker room at halftime. The whole joint looked big time.

When you got a real game sooner or later everybody peeps it and you don't show up nowhere like a stranger. When we came onto the court one of their players came over and asked which of us was Slam. I heard the dude popping the question and I had to smile. The truth is that my game is my fame and when I made the scene with my gangster lean I knew I was crazy good and on the money. We warmed up, running our lines and whatnot, and then the coach dropped the bomb on me. Nick and Trip were the starting guards. I put the ball down and left the warm-ups.

There was nothing for me to say so I don't say anything. I was definitely pissed. The way I saw it I earned my respect and I didn't go for him dissing me like I was some chump. He played me when he needed me and then let me sit when he thought he could get by without me like I was something he could just use and throw away. I didn't go for it.

The game started and Hunter could play. They were one of those teams that didn't do anything great but didn't blow anything either. If they had a deuce set up you could bank it. Nobody on their team was jamming or making any special moves. It was just pass, pass, move, cut, pass, and lay the sucker up. We were down 6 points, then we were down 9, and then 12 with a minute to play in the first half.

"Is the prima donna ready to play now?" The coach stands right in front of me looking down like he was something special.

"Cop a walk!"

"What did you say?"

"You heard me, man," I said. "Go on and lose the game!"

I got up and walked into the locker room. Yo, I knew I was wrong but I still walked. I didn't know if I was madder at the coach for playing with my mind or madder at myself for letting him play with it.

There was a folding chair in the corner and I sat on it and put a towel over my head. It felt like everything was coming down on me and I just wanted to shut everything out. A little while later the team came in and I heard somebody pull up a chair next to mine.

"Get away from me."

"You're right," Ducky was saying. "You should have been in the game. You're right."

"Yeah, get out of here."

Ducky patted me on the shoulder and moved away.

I thought if I even got up I might start crying or something. What I would have really liked to have happened was to let the coach come up and jump up in my face. Then I could light him up. Hitting him would blow everything for me, but it was almost like it didn't matter. He could blow everything for me anyway.

I heard him talking about the game, how Latimer had to put out a hundred and ten percent, that old-time movie bull. He must have seen that on the late late show. When the team went out for the second half they went out quiet.

Goldy came over to me and sat where Ducky had been sitting.

"You want to hear the rest of it?" he asked me.

"I'm off the team?"

"No, the rest of it is that if you go on to make it big in basketball he's going to tell the world how he helped you make it big," Goldy said.

I looked up at him. "How he gonna do that when I ain't even playing unless he know he can't win without me?"

"What do you want?" Goldy asked. "You want fair? How come a kid as streetwise as you seem to be is so naive when it comes to real life?"

"I don't want to hear your stuff, man," I said.

"Well, I owe you one thing," Goldy said. "And that's some advice. You're a good ballplayer, right?"

"Yeah."

"You know you almost let Brothers talk you out of it last week," he said. "And now you're going to let the coach talk you out of it, right?"

"I can't play if he doesn't put me in."

"He'll put you in this half," Goldy said. "Play for yourself. Go for it."

"Then he's going to think he got me to play hard by keeping me out the first half," I said.

"Now you got it," Goldy stood up. "And it's up to you to play for yourself and show what you can do."

"It's not right, man," I said.

"Are you hard enough to handle it, anyway?" Goldy asked. "Hard enough to do what's right for Slam?"

"Yeah, I'm hard enough."

"Get your attitude together and come on out for the game." Goldy turned and walked out of the dressing room.

By the time I got out the game had started. Goldy spoke to Mr. Nipper and he looked over at me. I looked down at the hardwood floor. What I had said in the dressing room sounded good, but I didn't know if I was hard enough to deal with the coach at all. I just didn't know.

On the court Trip got trapped in the corner and threw up a three that rimmed and came out. Hunter came back with a nice deuce on a backdoor play. Nick and Glen tried to trap along the sidelines and they called Glen for a foul. The coach spoke to Goldy and he came over and told me to go in for Glen.

"We're going with a three-guard offense," Goldy said. "Keep going for the basket, make them stop you. If they collapse on you it'll open it up for Trip and Nick."

Hunter inbounded the ball and started their passing routine. No good. I jumped out after a pass and when the guy pulled it back Nick took it away. We were downcourt in a heartbeat with Trip leading. Their forward came over and Trip passed the ball back to me trailing. I got it right and went up strong with their center coming over to block out for the bound. I slammed that sucker so hard it snapped through the net like a whip.

They turned the ball over on a traveling call. Trip got the ball and passed it inside to Jimmy. Jimmy threw up a hook that was short. I went up over their forward, snatched the bound, and bounce-passed it back to Jimmy. He took it right up. I checked the scoreboard and saw we were only down by 5.

Hunter called a time-out and we went to the bench. Ducky threw me a towel. The dude was happy, smiling and everything. He really wanted me to do good.

When time was in they kept four men down to inbound the ball. They kept their forward at half-court; in case we tried to trap they'd have a third man to get the ball across the mid-court line.

Once they got the ball across mid-court they went into a kind of a lame weave. I didn't get what they were doing right away but Nick called it out.

"They're stalling! They're stalling!"

It was too early in the half to get into a slow-down but that was what they were doing. Trip went after the ball and got called for a foul.

"That's four on Trip," Nick said.

"How many you got?" I asked him.

"Two."

They brought the ball back in and went back into their stall.

"Back off! Let them shoot," I called out. "They're scared to shoot."

Nick gave me a look but he backed off. Their guard stopped and held the ball. He watched the clock until it ran down to ten seconds and then he passed the ball off and held two fingers up.

They brought the ball into their center and two of them cut, crisscrossing near the foul line looking for somebody to lose their man for the ball.

I went off my man and went after their center. He was about six foot six and was all elbows and shoulders. He didn't expect me to get on him and he passed the ball over my head out to where his forward had drifted. Trip beat the guy to the ball and sprinted down the court. We were down by three.

They came back with a deuce on a short jumper and Nick threw the ball all the way downcourt to Frank who had laid back on the last play.

They missed their next shot and Jimmy got the board and flung it out to Nick who got it to me. I was coming down the side and their forward was on me. When I got to the hoop I saw the dude had me cut off. He went up with me and he went up strong. His fingers were higher than the ball and straining toward it so I pulled it down and stretched my body out and pushed the pill with my fingertips. I was on the other side of the hoop and watched the ball roll over the side of the rim for the deuce.

They kept their forward on me but I was stronger than he was. He was looking for finesse but I came after him with muscle. On defense he could jump as high as I could if I let him get set. I kept my body on him so he couldn't set himself for the leap or blocked him out with my elbow in his chest.

On offense he was giving me too much room. He didn't put his body on me even when we were right under the basket, so I had the move.

Nick was feeding me the ball from every angle and we were moving away from them. The best feed he did was when he went across the lane and brought it through his legs on a bounce pass. Soon as I got the ball I had one thing on my mind, a reverse slam. I went up strong, spun, and slammed the ball into the rim. The sucker bounced out almost to mid-court. Embarrassed.

But the thing was we had them. Nick played his best game ever and even Jimmy got a few baskets as we beat them by five. We had won other games, but beating Hunter in their fine gym felt good.

We showered and got dressed and headed for the subway because the Forensics Team was using the school bus. Goldy got to me in the locker room, telling me that I had showed character.

"You have to show the same character off the court," he said.

"Yo, man, you don't blow a chance to give up a lecture, do you?"

"You're only going to be here another year," Goldy said. "I have to take every chance I can get. See you tomorrow."

"What did the coach say?"

"He said we can't afford to fall behind when we play Carver," Goldy said.

"Yeah. Right."

Ducky's mom had came to the game and she took him home and me and Nick copped the subway uptown. We were laughing and going on about the game so much people must have thought we were drunk or something. It was just a good feeling. Then, when we hit 125th Street we saw this devastated-looking chick get on the train. It was cold but she was sweating and I knew she was a head. What she looked like most was a blackbird that was caught in the rain. The chick really looked pitiful and it got me down.

I pushed my mind back to the game and what Goldy was saying about dealing for myself when things weren't going that tough. It all sounded good but just because something sounded good it didn't mean it was easy. Sometimes it seemed that when you were into a thing with schools and officials or just about anything that wasn't happening in the hood you couldn't even figure out what you were going up against. It was like a game where everybody knew the rules but you.

Ducky had been a trip, slapping me on the back and smiling and everything. Thinking about having him for a friend made me think of Ice, too. It was getting to be easier hanging with Ducky than it was with Ice. Hanging with Ice was scary. I wanted to know more about Ducky but I knew I was looking away from finding out more about Ice.

CHAPTER SEVENTEEN

Grandma got out the hospital. My moms said she wasn't any worse but she wasn't any better, either. I didn't dig it too tough. It was like they were sending her home to die. I busted over to her place and she was sitting at the kitchen table. She had on a housedress that looked a lot too big for her.

"How you doing, boy?"

"You know me, Grandma," I said. "I'm always doing good. You know I started making that videotape for you. When I get it edited I'll bring it over and show it to you."

"How you doing in school?" she asked. "Your mama said you were having a little trouble."

"I just got to buckle down and hit the books," I said. "Get serious."

"There was a time they didn't even let black

people go to school." Grandma got up and started making tea. "I only went three months a year when I was little."

Me and Grandma had tea and then she told me about a little Puerto Rican nurse she had met in the hospital and how smart she had been.

"She called herself Estella," she said. "Ain't that a pretty name?"

"Yeah."

"That nurse was pretty, too," she said. "I asked her if she had a boyfriend."

"What she say?"

"She said she didn't have none as handsome as my grandson," Grandma said. She gave me a wink.

"Yo, Grandma, good looking out."

We rapped for a while more and Grandma kissed me at the door when I was leaving, but the visit got me in a bad mood. Being sick and being old is something you have to deal with, but it isn't something you have to like.

When I got to school it was like everybody had a chip on their shoulder. We had a paper due in English and Mr. Parrish collected them. I remembered that we had the paper due some time, but I forgot just when. Mr. Parrish is the kind of guy who always thinks somebody is dissing him because they don't do their homework. Like, you're supposed to give him his propers by going home and working on what he wants you to work on. Then if you show late he cops this nasty attitude and puts his mouth on you.

"So, Mr. Harris, just why *are* you taking up classroom space?" He was standing over me. "Why don't you just go out to your neighborhood and find a corner to stand on? That's what you want from life, isn't it?"

"Don't be standing over me, man," I said.

"Don't *be* standing over me?" he raised his voice. "Is that directly from your African background? Maybe from the We-Be tribe?"

As I got up I knew I was wrong. And I knew that what I had in mind was to rock his jaw. I pulled my fist back and felt somebody grab my arm. It was little Karen. By the time I had turned and pushed her away, Mr. Parrish had backed away and was headed toward the door.

"Forget him!" Karen was yelling at me. "He's wrong, forget him!"

My books were on my desk and I reached for them and knocked them to the floor. I left them there and walked on out the classroom. Mr. Parrish was already all the way down the hall, headed toward the principal's office. The door leading outside was in the other direction and I headed that way.

It was cold as it wanted to be. The hawk was biting and there were snow flurries in the air. There was a little restaurant down the street and I went into it and ordered a cup of soup.

"Seventy-five cents!" the guy behind the counter said.

"Yeah."

He took the change I put on the counter and I took the soup and found a table.

The soup was barley bean, which I don't dig that tough but it was hot and the restaurant was warm. I kept having flashes of scenes go off in my mind. Some scenes would have me punching out Mr. Parrish. Other scenes would have me being put out of school, or getting arrested. I tried to think back if I had hurt Karen. She looked okay, I thought. I wondered why she jumped up and grabbed me. Did I look like a wild man or something?

"So what's happening?"

I jumped when I heard Goldy's voice.

"You had trouble in Mr. Parrish's class?"

"Yo, man, he caught me wrong and I blew up," I said. "It's not a big deal."

"If you say so."

"I'm saying so."

"Who was right in the class just now?" he asked.

"I guess he was," I said. "He's the teacher and I'm just the student. No matter what he said I can't do nothing about it."

"He's down in the office now trying to get you suspended," Goldy said. "A couple of the kids from the class came down and spoke up for you."

"Yeah?"

"They don't hate you as much as you hate yourself, it seems." Goldy looked into my soup. "What's this?"

"Barley bean soup."

"Phew! I thought it was the coffee."

I had to smile. It was good hearing that some of the kids went and talked up for me. It was good Goldy came to the restaurant, too.

"How did you know I was here?"

"I didn't, I just looked around for you," Goldy said. "Tell me, Slam, why do you keep self-destructing? You find a way of making money at it or something?"

"This going to be one of your lectures?"

"No, why don't you make it one of your lectures," Goldy said. "Why don't you tell me what's going on? You know, I'm really interested."

"Why?"

"It's just something I don't understand," he

said. "It's not like you're the first kid that's been through Latimer who has trouble getting along. It happens once or twice every year. Some black kids, some white kids. Usually with the black kids it happens louder, more obviously, but it happens every year."

"Ask the white kids."

"I got you here now," Goldy said. "And I'll make a deal with you. You tell me what's going on, and I'll work with you to get you out of this mess with Mr. Parrish."

I looked at the dude. He looked sincere. Two girls came in smoking cigarettes. They saw Goldy and backed out real quick.

"You want me to cop a plea," I said, "and I don't know what to say."

"Just tell me what you think is wrong," he said. "And if you're not going to eat the soup . . ."

"Go ahead."

He started eating the soup and the guy behind the counter brought him over some crackers.

"Hey, how come you didn't bring me the crackers when I had the soup," I said. "I paid for it."

"You want crackers?"

"Forget it."

"So?" Goldy had a soup mustache.

"So everybody says I'm wrong, okay? I didn't do this, and I didn't do that. I messed up a test. I forgot my homework." The guy brought the crackers and another bowl of soup.

"On the house," he said.

"You get privileges being with a white guy," Goldy said.

"I'm hip."

"So go on."

"Then they start running this game about how when I get out of school I ain't going to be into nothing. That's what Parrish ran down. I was going to be a corner guy, you know, just hanging on the block 'cause I don't have anything going for me.

"He acts like I don't see nothing. You think I don't see the dudes on my block ain't doing nothing? He sees it and I see but when he throws it in my face he's not showing me any respect. Like, if I run up to him and said he's half bald and all ugly or something like that, then I'm not showing him respect. He knows he's half bald, and he knows he ain't no movie star, either. But if I throw that up in his face then everybody is going to say I'm dissing him. When he throws stuff up in my face I'm supposed to act like I'm happy with it. You know, 'Thank you Mr. Parrish for dissing me in front of the whole class because it's for my own good and I feel real glad that you did it.'"

"Is he right concerning your schoolwork?" Goldy asked.

"Yeah," I said. "He's right."

"So, say he was a ballplayer talking trash to you on the court," Goldy said. "What would you do? Punch him out?"

"If we were on the court I would have my game with me," I said. "I don't have a game off the court."

"You still don't get it, do you?" Goldy finished up his soup and took mine. "The only difference between on the court and off the court is that *everybody* is in the game off the court. You *will* play, and you *will* win or lose. There's nobody on the bench, nobody sitting it out. You're in the game, Slam. You're in it whether you want to be or not. A lot of people fool themselves and say they're just not going to play. Believe me, it don't work that way."

"How you know so much?"

"I'm guessing," Goldy said. "When I come back to life I'm coming back as Michael Jordan and then I'll try a different theory. Now let's get back to the school."

"You going to talk to Mr. Tate for me?"

"About what?"

"You said you would work with me to get me out of trouble," I said.

"You're not in trouble," Goldy said. "Once the kids took your side Parrish backed off. He's going to be looking for you to make a mistake, though. You know that, right?"

"Yeah, I guess I dissed him, too."

"You might even be learning something," Goldy said.

"Look, thanks for coming by and talking to me."

"I just do it for the soup," Goldy said.

We got back to the school and a few of the kids got to me and asked me what was going on. I told them it was no big deal. Then I had an idea. Tony said that Mr. Parrish was in the library, and I went there and found him. He had some books in his hands and he put them in front of his chest when I walked up to him.

"I'm sorry I blew up like that," I said. "It won't happen again."

He didn't know what to say. You could see it in his eyes. He was thinking a mile a minute and then he nodded and sort of mumbled "okay" under his breath.

When I got to math, Mr. Greene was waiting for me. He said he heard I was really a tough guy.

There wasn't any homework due and I was glad, but that didn't get Mr. Greene off my back. He kept on about how Mr. Parrish was a lot tougher than I even knew about.

"You tough, too?" I asked him.

"Tough enough to see that you don't graduate," he said. "How's that for tough?"

"That's pretty tough," I said. "Is that why you're a teacher, to see who you can stop from graduating?"

"No, I'm here to maintain standards of excellence," he came back. "Would you know anything about that?"

"I thought you were here to teach," Ducky said.

"Why don't you shut up," Mr. Greene said.

"You tough enough to keep me from graduating?" Ducky said.

Mr. Greene turned red and started the lesson.

He was right, though. He was tough enough to keep me from graduating. He was like Brothers on Trinity's team. He had a good game and he was talking trash. Goldy had said that there were going to be winners and losers, off the court as well as on, and I knew I didn't know what winning off the court was. That's what they should have been teaching us in math — how to win. Maybe that's why I had a good game on court, I knew how to win there.

When the last bell rang I felt drained. No way I wanted to go to basketball practice. In the locker room Glen and Trip were playing chess and somebody, probably Trip, had a radio on blasting out some reggae.

There was some three-inch tape on the table and I took a roll and wrapped my ankles. There was nothing wrong with them but I liked the way they felt when they were wrapped. Ducky was putting on his N.W.A. sweatshirt to practice in. Off the court he was pretty tough, too. You wouldn't think it looking at him, but he was.

Practice went good with most of it being about clogging up the middle. Everybody on Carver's squad could throw the pill down and that was a big part of their game.

"It's also a weakness." The coach was talking to us as we sat on the floor. "They throw away chances by looking for the slam, and looking for the one-on-one. They're generally a more athletic team than we are, but the points count the same if you do a three-sixty slam or if you hit two foul shots. Nick, I'm putting you on Reese, their best player."

"Why don't you put Slam on him?" Nick said. "He's the best player we have."

"I question whether or not he's the best player we have," the coach said. He picked up his clipboard again. "And we don't want to have this game breaking down into a two man jitterbug contest. We saw what happened against Trinity. We can win because we have the best team effort in the league."

I looked over at Goldy and he was looking dead at me.

We did some curls and half squats and then some wind sprints before the practice ended. Goldy ran some of the wind sprints with us and I asked him why.

"To show Nipper I'm mad at him for making that crack about jitterbugging," he said.

"You have a heart attack and die and he'll really know you're mad," I said.

When I got home I saw that Derek had picked up some fresh videotape because he wanted to tape himself singing.

"Yo, man, you can't sing," I said.

"You want to tape me doing push-ups?"

"No."

"What you want to do?"

"Come on with me and we'll see what we find," I said.

"We're like the NEWS-4 team, right?"

"Sure."

We walked down to a lot on Malcolm X Boulevard. Some homeless guys were in a vacant lot off 139th Street standing around a fire in a garbage can. I asked them if I could run some tape.

"Don't tape this side of me," the oldest guy said. "This is my bad side."

"Both your sides is your bad side." The tallest guy didn't have any teeth.

"You play ball?" the old guy asked.

"Yeah," I said.

"Go on and take your pictures," the old guy said. He turned his good side to me. "You got any money?"

"'Bout seventy-five cents," I said.

"Well, you keep it because you need it to chase the ladies," the old guy said.

"What kind of lady he gonna get for seventy-five cents?" the tall guy asked.

The fire flared up and lit their faces from underneath and I saw that they were all younger than I thought they were.

"If he a real man the ladies will give him money," the old guy said. "Ain't that right young blood?"

"You got it," I said.

A black cop came along and told them not to let the fire get out of hand. They said they wouldn't and he nodded and went on about his business. He did what he had to do and they did what they had to do. I guess they were in the game, too.

I told Derek that he had to carry the camera home because he was my assistant and he dug it. The way he was working his thing he was going to end up being my main man. When I got home I looked through the assignments and found the one I was supposed to do for Mr. Parrish. It was supposed to be a three-page paper showing how something that happened in one of Shakespeare's plays also happened in our own community. That was easy. I just used that scene in the beginning of Romeo and Juliet when those guys were dissing each other and then the scene where Romeo was talking his stuff to Juliet.

There was a roach on the wall of my room and I threw a sneaker at him but missed. Then I grabbed the other sneaker and chased him behind the closet. I stood right next to the closet for a while but he came out the other side and ran up the wall near the ceiling where he thought I couldn't get him. He must have been shocked to see me sky because he didn't even move. *Wham*! I didn't hit him, just gave him a good scare.

He was probably thinking to himself, Whoa, that dude can get up! But I wonder why they call him Slam?

I put the tape in the VCR and played it back. The raspy voice of the guy in the lot filled the living room. Derek came in and watched the tape. We didn't say anything about the guys. They were making jokes and all, but it wasn't funny.

CHAPTER EIGHTEEN

I went to school early so I could look over all the tapes. Miss Fowell, the librarian, was in the tape room.

"You guys have a big game tomorrow," she said.

"You watching basketball now?"

"Hey, I'm hurt," she said. "I've seen all of your home games. I used to play basketball in college."

"You?" I looked at her. "You got an athletic scholarship?"

"I didn't get a scholarship," she said. "But I played. St. Joseph's in Brooklyn."

"All right!"

"What are you doing?"

"Just some tapes from the neighborhood," I said.

"Don Parrish liked it a lot," she said.

"He doesn't like *me* a lot," I said. "We had a little run-in."

"I know, he was some pissed." She took a tape from the machine she was near. "But I think he was right. Just because you made a good videotape doesn't make you a good person."

"He still thinks the tape is good?"

"Yes, and so do I," she said. "But it won't do you a bit of good if you don't keep the rest of your life together."

"Yo, Miss Fowell, how come every adult in the world has a lecture they're just ready to give out?"

"You hear all of the lectures when you're young." She was putting labels on some new tapes. "When you get older you realize how many of them were really a lot more important than you knew."

"So you lay it on some kid?"

"Now you got it," she said. "So, you guys going to win tomorrow?"

"It won't be easy," I said. "But we'll do it."

"Good luck."

"Yo, you coming?" I called after her as she was going out the door.

She stuck her head back in and put her thumb up.

I didn't even know she knew anything about basketball.

The tapes looked good, or at least I thought they did after what Miss Fowell said. While I was watching them I thought about Mr. Parrish getting on my case, and still saying that I was okay as a moviemaker.

The tapes didn't look like a movie to me. What they looked like was just pictures of the block. They made me laugh sometimes when I saw people I know showing out for the camera. Yeah, I dug that.

Marjorie had nutted up when she saw the first tapes. That was okay, it wasn't her show. It was my show and my turf and pictures of my homies. The houses only looked bad when you compared them to houses you see on television and whatnot. They weren't anything grand, and the people weren't anything grand, but they were okay with me. Square business. It looked like if I put it together and cut it down like Mr. Parrish said, it would definitely be on the money. I was hoping he would still be interested in helping me.

When I put in the tape of Carver playing Trinity it was just like television. I could follow the ball good and all it needed was for somebody to announce it.

"Ice puts the ball on the floor, he fakes left, then goes left and leaves Brothers

228

standing in his tracks. He looks away, then goes up and rips the net with a bodacious slam!"

I watched Ice some more. His game was smoking. Brothers was smiling and laying off him. He didn't want to look bad when Ice went around him, over him, and just about through him. Brothers should have stayed on Ice and made him bring his weight for the whole game. A little knot grew in my stomach and I knew I was getting an excitement buzz.

In art we had to do a portrait from memory. I thought about doing a portrait of Ice but instead I did a portrait of Mtisha. I did it with pastel crayons on really good paper Mr. Kenny, the art teacher, brought in.

"Concentrate on what you notice most about your subject," Mr. Kenny said.

What I noticed most about Mtisha was how she made me feel. She made me feel warm so I started off with a warm brown color even though she was darker than the shade I was using. I got her eyes pretty good and the top of her nose real good. From there it was like just filling out her face. She was wearing her hair in braids but I didn't want to draw braids so I changed her hairstyle. I didn't want to draw her smile, either, because I thought I was going to mess that up, but I didn't.

When I painted in the curve of her mouth I was surprised how nice her lips were. Then I knew that maybe I wasn't even seeing the picture, maybe I was just looking at the paper and seeing Mtisha in my mind.

"This is obviously somebody you like a lot?" Mr. Kenny asked.

"Yeah, you can say that," I said.

"Nice technique," he said. "Nice feeling to the piece. You need to look at her skin more and see all the other colors in it. Nobody's skin is just one color. Add any warm color to it and you'll see what I mean."

"Yeah, okay."

The skin tones were a little flat, but they were good enough to bring my mind big time to Mtisha.

The rest of the day went by quick and Mr. Tate called a special pep rally at two-thirty for the big game with Carver. The whole school was there and they were getting up for it. We got into our uniforms and threw the ball around the stage a few times and each player was introduced and got a cheer. I was glad when my man Ducky got his cheer.

"Yesterday Trinity lost." The coach was talking over the loudspeaker. "What that means is that only Carver is undefeated. But Carver isn't in a very good position because they have to play us!"

Everybody got to screaming behind that and the band started playing our school song, which sounded like everybody else's school song.

"When they lose to us tomorrow afternoon we will both be five and one, but we will be the conference champions because we will have beaten the second-place team, Carver. We win tomorrow and it's on to the citywide Tournament of Champions!"

There were more cheers and the band got louder than I knew it could get. What the coach didn't say was that if we won and got into the Tournament of Champions the first team we would have to face was Carver, the defending champs.

When the rally was over we changed into our street clothes and me, Ducky, Nick, and Jimmy stopped for a soda across the street. We didn't say a whole lot, just some weak stuff about how the game was going to be good and all. What was more important was that we didn't say anything negative. I thought about saying something about being sorry about the fight before, but figured I would just let it lay.

Outside I saw Goldy waiting to cross the street. He had on this knit cap and black overcoat.

"You look like a bank robber, man," I said to him.

"You nervous about the game tomorrow?" he asked.

"Not really," I lied.

"Good, then you won't mind that the game is being taped, and that twelve colleges called and asked for copies of the tape," Goldy said. "No big deal, right?"

"No lie?"

"They want to see Ice against some competition," Goldy said. "You're it."

"Nick's going to be on Ice."

"Between you and me I think that the coach got a few calls and made a few promises," Goldy said. "Make sure you bring a clean jock strap, people will be watching."

CHAPTER NINETEEN

"So your team ready to go down?" Ice stood with me in the middle of the floor as our teams warmed up. Some photographers were taking our picture and I tried to ignore them. We were playing at our gym but the stands had as many Carver fans as Latimer fans.

"They think they're going to win," I said.

"Why they think that dumb stuff?" Ice asked, grinning.

"I guess I told them," I said.

Ice cracked up and I laughed, too. Nothing was funny, the thing was that Ice was trying to get to my head. He pointed to me and laughed. Then he gave me five and went on back over to his team.

"Okay, we've got to make them work for what they get," the coach said. "Jose, Jimmy, their center is good and he's taller than we are. You've got to keep him out of the low post. Push him out, make him work. I'll work the refs to get some three-second violations. That way they can't just park in the paint. Slam, you're going to be on your pal Ice and you need to keep the ball away from him. You do that by playing him when he doesn't have the ball."

He didn't say anything about Nick guarding Ice, or even about changing. Goldy was right. Somebody dropped a dime and the coach picked up the phone.

When I go into a big game I always try to do at least one thing right away. Sometimes I try to slam. Sometimes I try to stuff the dude I'm holding so he knows who's the boss. Against Ice it was different. Brothers hadn't worked him, hadn't stayed on his case. I decided to just make sure he brought all his weight on every play.

They got the tip and Ice had the ball. He pointed at me and started to move toward midcourt. Ice could go either way and I knew it. He faked left and came right and I eased off of him. He was too far from the hoop to do anything serious.

He passed the ball to the off guard and got it back and started dribbling between his legs. It looked good but he wasn't going anywhere with it.

Then he made a strong move down the right side of the lane with me right with him. He brought the ball up, then pulled it down and laid it against the backboard on the other side for a reverse layup.

"He can't stop it," he said to his center loud enough for me to hear.

Nick brought the ball down against Joe Fletcher, their other guard. Joe was one of those little guys who looked like they got five arms, all reaching for the ball. I set a pick at mid-court and Nick tried to run him into it but he slid through.

When Fletcher got away from the pick I released and started across the key. Ice was on me, and he kept his elbow in my side. I pushed him back just as I heard the crowd cheer. Fletcher had stolen the ball from Nick and was off for a breakaway goal. They were up four to nothing.

"I bet we beat you by twenty points." Ice was in my face running his mouth. "What you think?"

I brought the ball down and Ice was pushing me with his fingertips. Not hard, not enough for the ref to call a foul, but enough to throw me off. Nick tried to set a pick but when I got near it Fletcher jumped off him and double-teamed me. I went up to throw the ball to Nick, who was open, but Ice was all over it.

He grabbed the ball, spun, and threw it over his

shoulder to Fletcher who was already going down-court. They were up by six.

We needed something and we needed it quick. Jose inbounded the ball to Glen who brought the ball up. Ice was running his mouth in my ear a mile a minute. I went to the boards and told Frank to move out. When Ice saw what I was doing he tried to get position on me. Nick drove down the left side, stopped, and went up like he was going for the short jumper. He passed the ball in to me and I went up with Ice all over me. The ball went off the backboard in the net and I pushed Ice off as we came down.

"Don't get nasty on me," he said. No, he didn't just say it, he hissed it at me.

"Shut up and play," I said.

Their center scored the next two baskets and our coach called a time-out.

"You guys are playing tight," the coach said. "You got to have fun, loosen up."

Nobody on our team was talking. They were tight, and they didn't think they were going to win.

"How we look?" I asked Ducky.

"Bad," he said.

We started back out onto the floor and Nick

told Jose to set picks near the mid-court line when we were bringing the ball up.

"No, man." I put my hand on Jose's arm. "Don't give in to them. If they steal the ball, they just steal it. We're as good as they are."

Nick gave me a look like he didn't like what I was saying. I couldn't beat Carver by myself, I needed the whole team coming out strong.

Glen brought the ball down and threw a bullet pass in to Jose. It went off Jose's hands and Ice got it. But then Nick picked the ball off by coming from behind Ice as he went downcourt. Nick came downcourt fast and passed it off to Jose who threw up a little hook. Their center knocked it away and I got it at the foul line. Ice came out on me but he came too close and I went around him. He cut off their center when he caught up with me but I was already on the way up. I threw it down hard and our side of the gym let out a roar.

The ball came in to Ice and he never stopped. He went up and slammed with me hanging on his arm, but the ref didn't call the foul. Ice complained and the ref told him to play ball.

Nick threw in a three-pointer and Fletcher brought the ball down for Carver. The game was going too fast. They were running up and down the court and I knew we weren't going to run with them.

Fletcher had the ball and Ice was looking for the pass. I dogged him strong and he didn't like it. He tried to cut around the baseline looking for a back door play or maybe to post me up low. When he did that I put my hand on his hip and leaned on him. He pushed me hard right in front of the ref but the ref didn't blow the whistle. They were letting us play through.

Fletcher got the ball in to their center who threw up a hook that bounced around the rim before falling through.

Coach had seen the same thing I did and called a time-out. He took out Frank at forward and brought in Trip; we were going to play the three-guard offense again.

The Carver coach pointed at Trip.

"He's too small! He's too small!" he called out.

Trip came in ready. He brought the ball down and their forward was trailing him. He faked a pass and their forward went for it as Trip threw up a short jumper for the deuce.

They posted Trip low and their forward took him right up. We got the ball and I missed an easy shot and they brought the ball down again. I was in Ice's face, cutting him off wherever he went. He was playing stronger, putting some muscle on me and talking stuff.

Fletcher missed a short jumper but their center put it back up and in.

Nick called a play for me. It was a double pick at the top of the key. When I got the pill Ice had his hand on my leg. He fought through the first pick but the second one got him. I thought I was too deep to slam so I just laid it up. Good thing, too, because Ice was over the rim waiting for me to get up. When he came down he was mad.

The rest of the first half went the same way. Me laying on Ice, and Trip and Nick working on Fletcher. It didn't stop them, but it slowed them down and sometimes it confused them. At the end of the first half it was Carver 31 and Latimer 23. Ice, with me steady on his case, had still scored 15 points.

In the locker room we were exhausted. The coach was saying we had played good, and Goldy was all excited.

"You have to know that this is the best I've ever seen them play," he was saying. "They're the City Champions, they're playing their best ball and we're still in this game. We're still in it."

"Ice is good," Ducky said. "He can do anything."

"Tell me about it," I said.

I remembered what Ice had done to Brothers. He had made him look bad until the end of the game. Then Brothers had looked okay. Either Ice had got tired or he had eased off Brothers.

We came out for the second half and Ice came up to me again.

"You trying hard, huh?" he said.

"Got to try hard against you," I said.

"Maybe you can play this half without leaning all over me," he said, still smiling.

He was smiling but I knew he meant it.

They got the tip and Fletcher had the ball. I made a point of stepping on Ice's foot and he gave me a look. Then he pushed off and got the ball and went strong for the hoop. I had the half step but I knew what he was going for. One step past the foul line and he took off for the slam.

You can't stop no slam with your fingers between the ball and the basket unless you want to get your fingers busted up. You have to hit the ball from the side and hope he hasn't got his wrist cocked to power it through. I pushed the ball and Ice slammed it into the back rim. The ball come out and their forward grabbed it and threw up a jumper that missed and Jose tapped it out to Trip.

We came down and Nick threw up a trey that fell. Ice called for the ball and told his team to clear. They cleared and Nick came over and double-teamed Ice. Good looking out. But then Ice made a spin move like he was going into Nick, then head-faked back toward me and went left hard. It left me and Nick running into each other at the top of the key.

That move would have discouraged me and might have really got me down if Nick hadn't picked up his game big time. He started going after everything. If he went down he wasn't going down lame.

The coach signaled up to play a box-and-one defense. On offense we lost the ball on a backcourt violation. We fell into the box-and-one with the rest of the team playing the zone box and me on Ice. Jose and Glen played deep. Nick and Trip played high, and I kept dogging Ice.

I could feel Ice was getting mad. When they called time-out and he started toward the bench I stepped in front of him.

"What's wrong with you, man?" He looked at me.

I threw him a grin and he sucked his teeth and walked away.

When I play scrub ball I just do my thing and

don't worry about it. But when I'm playing against somebody really tough I start looking for the inch. If I can get up an inch higher than my man I can do something he can't do, if I can reach an inch further than he can I can get to the ball first. But when you're reaching like that, straining for the ball, you start to tense up and then you can't do anything with the ball even if you do get it.

I was reaching for the ball, busting every play, and trying not to tense up. I had to keep my eyes on the pill and keep going for it and keep making the moves even when I wasn't hitting. We were coming back slowly but time was running out.

Carver was pushing Jimmy around good but Nick was on the case and whenever Jose was in he was tougher even though he wasn't as quick as Jimmy.

Ice was playing me hard but I was getting to his stuff. At first it was just a fingertip or a nail, and then it was the top of my finger. He stopped trying to get over me and started freaking, bringing the ball down and around his back. But the ref wasn't calling touch fouls and Nick and Trip were helping out anytime Ice went up in the air and brought the ball back down.

His catch-up step was quick and never slowed

down. A couple of times he caught me when I thought I had the step on him but I was going up stronger than he was. I didn't know how good I was playing him, but I thought it was even. He wasn't kicking my butt and I wasn't kicking his. But then, halfway through the second half, he stopped dogging me. He yelled for a switch one time when he could have slipped through a pick and I found myself alone, unchallenged for the first time in the game. I went up with both hands on the ball and jammed it through. When I turned back Ice was looking away. It was like he had tried me and now was going someplace else.

We caught up with Carver on a pretty play by Trip. He came down with their guard all over him. He went baseline, faked a straight layup, and then hit the reverse. There were two minutes to play. We each had one time-out. They took Ice out and our coach took me out, which I didn't like.

"They're giving him a few-seconds breather," the coach said. "He's their crunch man. They're looking to bringing it down to one play."

They stalled around, trying to set up a play, and finally got the ball in to their center who had positioned Jimmy deep. Jimmy grabbed him as he started to go up and the ball went straight up in the air. The ref blew the foul as their center turned and grabbed Jimmy by the throat. We jumped in and broke them apart before it became a fight.

It was a two-shot foul and their center, a big guy who looked like George Foreman, blew the first shot and made the second.

Trip came down and hit Glen on a backdoor play and we were up by one.

The game clock read one minute and ten seconds. They brought Ice back in and I came in to guard him.

The rest might have done him some good but I was so excited it didn't mean a thing to me. Fletcher brought the ball down for them, cut across the paint, and threw up a shot that Jose slapped away. The ball was on the floor and me and Ice went for it. It was going toward the sidelines and I got my fingers on it but Ice slapped it back the other way and was on it in a flash. His whole body was slanting and he was moving across the court. I was a whole step behind him, looking for some help. Glen jumped out as Ice went up. Ice slammed over him and pointed at him as he came down. They were up by one.

The clock read fifty seconds. Nick was bringing the ball down and I started down the sidelines. Ice put his hand on my chest and started holding, making me fight my way through him.

Yeah, okay. I went into him, spun around, planted my elbow in his chest, and pushed off toward the hoop. I looked up and saw the ball coming and went up for it. Nick had thrown the ball for the alley-oop but it was off and I had to reach for it. It was on my palm off to the side, and I curled my body as I turned and pushed the ball around their center toward Jose. Jose went up for the layup, took a shot in the mouth, but made that sucker. We were up by one.

I started downcourt when Trip stopped me. The ref had called a foul on the shot.

Jose's mouth was bleeding when he went to the line and his eyes were puffy. He bounced the ball hard.

"It's yours, Jose!" Glen called to him.

The coach had give us a saying when we were on the line. Heels up, knees bent, soft shot, red hot. Jose's heels were up, he bent his knees, and put the ball up. It took forever to reach the rim but it fell through. We were up by a deuce.

Their center brought the ball down. Ice was deep and I thought he was going to try to post me. The center passed the ball off to Fletcher. Ice popped out and got the quick pass. He pointed at me, made a move to his left, changed direction once, twice, and then did a stutter step which got my feet turned. He flew by me and went for the hoop. I started to go for the stop but I didn't want to foul him. I brought both hands back so the ref could see that I didn't foul him as he tied the score.

There were fourteen seconds left.

Trip brought the ball down for us. I told myself not to look at the clock. I looked. There were nine seconds left when the ball came across the mid-court line. Ice had his hands on me again. I leaned on him and he spread his legs to keep me from pushing him away. The spin didn't shake him and I saw Fletcher double-team Trip. Trip tried passing to Nick but their center slapped the ball back. Ice had released me when the ball was on the floor, so when Nick grabbed it and threw it over his shoulder I was free. I had to jump for the pill and when I came down Ice was in my face and going for the pill. I faked a jump and he slapped the ball. Not hard enough. I held onto it and went up for the jumper. The ball was on my palm over my head with my elbow pointed toward the rim and my wrist cocked. Somebody grabbed my shirt at the waist as I started the shot. It felt like my shoulder was coming out of the socket as I felt myself being pulled down. My fingers touched Ice's fingers in midair as the ball floated over him. The next thing I knew I was on the floor and Nick was on top of me screaming and pounding me with his fists. We had won!

The teams shook hands and Ice was cool. He put his arm around my neck and we had our pictures taken together. We were homies, and everything was everything between us, but I had won.

"You want to party tonight?" he asked as the teams were headed for the locker room.

"Where you going to party?"

"My crib. I'll call you," he said. "You going to be home?"

"Tired as I am? Best believe it."

"You came out smoking today," he said. "I didn't think you could get that serious."

"Nothing beats a try," I said.

"Call you tonight."

"Bet."

In the locker room the guys were going crazy. Two girls from the band were in there and five teachers, including Miss Fowell. They were hugging us and stuff.

The thought came to me that we had won, and

maybe they wouldn't have been there if we had lost. Maybe that was something to think about for the off-court game, too.

Ducky came over and poured a cup of soda over my head. That was a stupid-butt thing to do, but I was so happy to win it didn't make a bit of difference.

CHAPTER TWENTY

Sometimes when something good happens to me I can't wait to get off by myself so I can think about it. Goldy came up to me after the game and hugged me, the coach hugged me, teachers were hugging the whole team. It was like a fantasy trip. Moms had went to visit Grandma but Pops and Derek were there.

"Man, you guys played up some ball!" Pops said. He was looking around at everybody congratulating me and I knew he was digging it. I was digging him digging it, too.

Then Derek grabbed me and took me over to some of his friends to show off and I was high-fiving some little dudes with stick hands.

The locker room was crazy good. The smell of sweat and funky socks was all over the place and guys were screaming just to hear themselves screaming. Nick grabbed me around the neck and I held his hand up and pointed to him.

"Here he is!"

"Here we are!" the coach said. "Here we are!"

I hung out for a while, soaking it all up, and then I went on home. Moms was watching television and Derek was trying to get the wheel of his bicycle straight.

"Hi, star!" Moms said. "I heard you won."

"On the money," I said. "Anything around to eat?"

"The food's on the stove," Moms said. "I'll fix you a plate."

"How's Grandma?" I said.

"She's looking good," Moms said. "Being out of the hospital has done her good."

Pops ran down his version of the game as I ate. Dude didn't know nothing about ball, but he meant well.

I went and laid across my bed. The day came down on me hard. My legs felt like stone and my shoulders were aching. The game was still running through my mind, almost slipping into a real dream, when Moms came to the door.

"Mtisha's on the phone," she said.

Derek had his wheel all apart again, and I had to step over it. He needed to take the wheel to the bicycle shop and get it aligned with the machine they had down there.

"What's happening?" I asked when I picked up the phone.

She said that Bianca was inviting us to Ice's house to a party. "Come on over," Mtisha said. "And don't wear your sneakers."

"Why she invite me to go with you?" I asked. "She don't know who I want to bring to the party."

What did I say that for? She came on with I didn't have to take her to a party and how she could find someone to go with if she did want to go.

"Hey, I didn't mean anything," I said. "I'm playing around, that's all." Then I told her to lighten up and she told me she would see me when she saw me and just because I won a basketball game didn't mean I had the right to go around hurting people.

After she hung up I called her back and told her I was sorry, even though I really didn't think I did anything wrong.

"I'll see you over at Ice's place," I said. "And no matter what you say I still love you."

"You better be ready to prove it," she said, and hung up.

What did she mean by that? What was she going to do? I imagined her whispering some nice little things in my ear. Supposed she told me to go back to her house with her? Suppose she even asked me to marry her? I didn't think she would go that far, but how far would she go?

When I got to Ice's house the place was jumping. There were at least thirty people there, including some really fly women. They had a deejay with one of those twin turntables playing some tough sides. Ice and Bianca saw me and came over.

"You know you got to face us again in the Tournament of Champions, right?" he said.

"Yeah, I know," I said.

"So that's why we giving this party," he said. "So you can enjoy yourself one last time before the slaughter."

"I'm giving this jam because I needed to bring my good friends together," Bianca said. "But you guys can talk all the basketball you want just as long as you don't bring my party down. Mtisha said she'd be here soon."

Basketball's my game but I can rock a dance session. Bianca gave me a little kiss on the cheek and introduced me to some folk. There weren't any hip-hoppers on the set and nobody wearing gang colors. I dig a conservative set and I was doing my thing on the floor when Mtisha showed. She was wearing white pants and a soft white sweater that was just a stone killer outfit and she knew it. She looked at me and she had to smile because she knew she was making my mind go soft around the edges.

Mtisha showed cool and me and her and Ice and Bianca got out on the floor and improvised a little four-way number. If it was as good to see as it was to feel we would have got a Grammy Award or something. Then everybody was on the floor and the beat got as righteous as it could get. That's when I remembered about Mtisha saying that I had better be ready to prove my love. I decided then and there to make a serious move on the girl.

Ice's mama, Mrs. Reese, had a bag and was on her way out. She told us all to be good. She was going to stay at her cousin's house.

"I can't stand all that noise you children make," she said.

You could see that she was happy that Ice was having the party at home. She had probably spent all day cleaning the place so it would look nice.

Ice had a big corn-bread-and-collard-greens dude named Latin on the door to keep out the crashers. Everybody knew Latin was gay, but he played on Carver's football team and nobody was going to mess with him.

"So what I need to do to prove my love to you?" I asked Mtisha during a slow jam.

"I don't know," Mtisha said, sliding against me. "Slay some dragons or something."

"I think you're already in love with me," I whispered in her ear.

"I'm a little light-headed but I think it's a touch of the flu," she said. "Put your lips on my neck and see if I have a fever."

Latin brushed by and I saw him say something to Ice. The two of them started making their way through the party toward the front door. Bianca dug what was going down and you could see her face working like something was trying to get out. I pushed my mind away from it.

"What you want to do after the party?" I asked Mtisha.

"I told you I'm sick," she said. She didn't see what was going on. "I need to be taken care of."

"Whoa, look . . ."

We heard a banging against the door and everybody turned to look. Bianca turned the jam off and we heard scuffling outside the door.

"It's a fight!" somebody said.

Latin come in and he was waving that everything was cool.

"Some girl got drunk," he said. "She come off the street drunk and wanted to get into the party. No sweat."

The guy put the record back on and people started dancing again. I looked over to Bianca and her eyes was like wild panic. I knew what she was thinking.

"I got to find Ice," I told Mtisha.

Latin was getting a drink and nobody was on the door when I went out. In the hallway there were doors open and faces looking out to see what had happened. One guy in his bathrobe was on a cellular phone and I figured he was talking to the police.

The stairs were wide and I could see down the stairwell pretty good. It looked empty so I started down. I got all the way to the first floor and I didn't see anything. I looked out in the street and there were a few people standing around, but no big deal.

I raced back upstairs where Bianca was out in the hallway.

"Ice down there?" she asked.

"I didn't see him," I said. "Stay with the party, I'll find him."

Where was Ice? We were on the fourth floor and there were only five floors. I went up to the next landing and there wasn't anybody there either.

The roof door was open and I went outside. The cool breeze felt good. Ice was standing near the lit-tle wall that divided one roof from the other. On the edge of the roof, overlooking the street, was this chick.

"She's on the pipe!" Ice said.

The girl looked at me. In the rooftop darkness I couldn't see her good but I could see she was brown-skinned and skinny. Her eyes were shiny and desperate and her lips was drawn back from her teeth.

"Can you help me?" she asked.

"What you want?"

"She want some rocks," Ice said, before the girl could speak. "I don't know why she come here."

"Why you so near the edge?" I asked her.

"I just need to get straight tonight," she said. "I got a job in the morning."

For a minute I thought she might have been the girl I had seen on the subway, but I knew they all looked the same, scary and dried up and thrown away. She wavered on the edge of the roof and I thought she might fall, or even jump.

"I got a few dollars," I said. I started going through my pockets looking for money to give to her.

Ice held out his hand to her and opened it, palm up. I saw two plastic vials, the kind I had seen a hundred times in the gutter, in the park, in the bathrooms in school, everywhere in my life. The girl came away from the edge and grabbed the vials from Ice. She brushed past me as she went toward the door to the stairway.

"I don't know why she come to my party . . ." Ice come to me and put his arm around my shoulders.

I pushed him away hard.

"What's your problem?" he asked.

"Get away from me." I went to walk away from him and he jumped in front of me again.

"What's your problem?" he shouted the words at me.

"What don't you know? You dealing ain't you? You part of the life ain't you?" I could feel my neck swelling up with anger. "What don't you know?"

"Man, I can't help it if she's on the pipe," he said.

I didn't want him in my face and I pushed him away hard. He pushed me back and I swung on him. Ice fell back and then came after me.

"Punk!"

He had quick hands and went upside my head. I grabbed him around his waist, lifted him off the ground and threw him down. He got up as I tried to get past him and grabbed my shirt. I lifted my arm in time to stop him from hitting me again and he grabbed me around the neck.

He kept calling me a punk and tried to get me down. I wasn't going down. No way. I got my hand around his leg and lifted him again. There were some other people on the roof and I heard them yelling. They were pulling us apart and Ice tried to kick me. Latin picked me up and carried me off.

"Punk!" Ice called after me.

"What they fighting for?" somebody was asking.

"Slam, what's happening, man?" It was Billy from the bike shop.

"Nothing," I said.

I turned back to where Ice stood. He looked at me and I could see the anger in his face. I had peeped him. I had peeped him and it had messed with him good.

"You a punk!" he said. His voice was hoarse and cracking. "You a punk!"

"Yeah, man." I said. "That's me."

"Yo, Slam." Latin was by my side. "Y'all friends, man. Peace out. Both of you be cool in the morning."

Bianca was standing near the door of the roof and she touched me on the arm as I went by her. I went on downstairs and I heard Mtisha calling after me. There were some bloods standing around,

258

doing nothing as usual, and I just went on by them. My legs were trembling and I sat on the curb to get myself together.

"Bianca and I saw the girl," Mtisha said, sitting next to me.

"Yeah."

"Ice hurt you?" she asked.

"No, I'm okay. Just tired."

She moved closer and held my arm. "I know he hurt you," she said. She was crying softly.

Mtisha cried for a long time. She was right. Ice had hurt me. We had been aces for so long, had been playing ball and running the streets for so long that we knew each other's moves. We knew what we could do, and where we were going, and in a way, even how much we were hurting. Ice had hurt me, and he knew it. That's why he was hurting so much himself up there on the roof.

Mtisha had some money and we flagged down a cab.

"I just can't go home, right now," I told her.

"Baby, you need some rest," she said. "We can talk tomorrow."

We got to her house and I walked her upstairs. Her mother got upset when she saw that Mtisha had been crying but she was glad to see her safe.

I started down the stairs when Mtisha called me She come down a flight of stairs to me. She give me a kiss and five dollars.

"Get a cab," she said. "Be safe, baby."

When I got home it was like my whole head was going to explode. Moms wanted me to talk about it, but I didn't have enough words to say how I felt. Bad wasn't enough. Terrible wasn't even enough.

CHAPTER TWENTY-ONE

When I got to the school the next day the first thing I saw was a big banner that said CHAMPS. Some kids in the hallway started clapping and I wondered what was going on.

"Slam, I didn't see the game, but I heard you guys were great," Linda Yu said.

"The game?"

Mr. Tate came over. He stopped in front of me and put both hands on my shoulders. "I'm proud of you," he said. "The whole school is proud of you."

They were talking about the basketball game. Ice wasn't even in their world. People who didn't know nothing about no ball were up in my face saying how good it was that Latimer had won. When I got to math it was the same game. We were winners. Carver was a loser. That's all they were talking about.

The day dragged on. Once in a while I though

about trying to tell somebody about Ice, that he had been my friend, and that he was dealing. I remembered something I had heard about Malcolm X. He had said that when he was preaching on the corners in Harlem he was fishing for the dead. As far as I was concerned that's what Ice was, one of Harlem's dead. Even with his beeper which let him know who was trying to contact him, and his wheels which let him style around, he was in a kind of grave.

I didn't really think anybody else was going to understand what had went down except to say it was a ghetto thing. Like, you live there and you got roaches and you got crack and you got streets that don't get cleaned up and you got people giving up on life and that's what it's all about.

The coach called us together and told us that we'd be starting the citywide tournament during February.

"We can't live in the past," he said. "You all showed a lot of heart last night, but that win won't help us tomorrow. All that showed us is what we can do if we put our hearts and minds to it. The first practice will be Monday afternoon. And guys, be ready to do some serious work."

Yeah.

During the day the left side of my face swoll up. That was where Ice had hit me. I had a few day-dreams about punching him out, but I let it go pretty quick.

I told Ducky about the fight. I didn't tell him about Ice dealing. Maybe he would have under-stood it, but I felt ashamed to even say it. He knew I was upset about the fight and said that every-thing would probably turn out all right.

"Things have a way of working themselves out," he said. He was still wearing that stupid scarf.

When I got home there was a message on the re-frigerator to call Mtisha. There was a can of soda in the fridge and I grabbed it before calling.

"Bianca came to my house talking about how Ice is giving up messing with crack," Mtisha said. "She was saying we could all meet and talk it out."

"What you think?"

"What *you* think?" she came back.

"It don't matter what he says," I said. "We'll see what he's going to do. And the way I feel I don't want to hang with him to find out. You know what I mean?"

"Yeah, I'm mixed," Mtisha said. "Bianca is messed around bad because Ice is her old man and she wants to stick with him."

"So she wants to believe him when he says he's through?"

"Yeah. You want to believe but it's hard," Mtisha's voice was soft on the phone. "Sometimes I think all you guys are just heartbreaks waiting to happen. It's scary."

"Yeah," I said. "But ain't nothing to do but deal with it."

"You going to call him?"

"No," I said. "I don't think I'd have anything to say."

In school Mr. Parrish asked me to show my video one day after school. I said yes and asked Mtisha to come and she said she would.

Marjorie had helped me edit the tape and it didn't jerk around as much as it did before. On the tape the buildings looked more crowded than they did when you actually saw them. There was the whole hood. The Gates of Prayer church, Sam's Fish Box, Ed's Armature, Akbar's, and Carl's Curio. There were all the people I had known most of my life, smiling in front of the camera because they knew I wouldn't diss them.

It was dark in the Media Center and Mtisha moved closer to me when the first shot of Ice came on. He was standing on the corner near the beauty shop, his arm around Mtisha, looking cool. I had to turn away from the screen when he was on. I knew the tape ended with the kids from the hood, some boys playing ball, some babies playing on the stoop, a long shot of some young girls jumping rope in front of the bicycle shop. I remembered looking down at them from the edge of the roof.

The coach was calling me Slam in practice and he was working us all hard. I was pushing it, too, dealing as hard as I could. I felt comfortable in the gym, safe. Basketball was my game. On the court I was good, maybe not as good as Ice, but I was getting there. I wondered how it would be to go up against him again. In my mind he was different, he had laid down when it was time to get up. He had his game, the same game I had, and I had thought the game would make us all right. It hadn't.

What I wished was that things would stop for a while and maybe we could all catch a breath and check out the score or something. That wasn't happening. What was happening was that the clock was still running, like Goldy had said it would, and we had to keep on keeping on the best way we could.

The coach ran a play where I was supposed to run Nick into a pick and then I would be free down the left side of the lane. The ball came to me and I put a head fake on Nick, did a stutter step, switched the ball to my left hand, and ran him toward the pick. Nick fought through and had his hand on my waist. He was on me until I went up, until I could feel the seams of the ball on my fingertips, until I could see the hoop in front of me and my wrist snapping the ball through the net and my fingers sliding off the smoothness of the rim.

"That's the way to work, Slam!" the coach called to me. "That's the way!"

Yeah. Okay. Maybe that was the way to work it. Maybe if I could get my game right, all my game, on and off the court, I would get over.

The coach called a play for Jimmy and he tried to post me, to push me deep into the paint so he could use his height against me. It wasn't going to happen. He pushed back, and when he couldn't move me he turned and gave me a look. I didn't say anything to him, but he knew who he had ran into, somebody too strong to be moved. He had ran into Slam.

About the Author

WALTER DEAN MYERS is the author of many highly acclaimed books for young adults, including *Motown and Didi: A Love Story, The Young Landlords, Slam!,* and *Somewhere in the Darkness,* all winners of the Coretta Scott King Award; *Scorpions,* a Newbery Honor Book; and *Monster,* a National Book Award Finalist, a Coretta Scott King Honor Book, and winner of the Michael L. Printz Award.

Walter Dean Myers's travels have taken him to the Far East, South America, and the Arctic. He presently lives in Jersey City, New Jersey. He is a member of the Harlem Writers Guild.

For the Best in Literature